THE CLAIM-JUMPERS

The hills outside Jackpot were full of gold and the town was full of miners, hoping to get rich. But if they struck paydirt they were given the choice of either getting out of town, or of filling a grave on Boot Hill. Even Sheriff Ryker couldn't catch the band of killers they called the Boot Hill Gang. Then the Preacher rode into Jackpot and, with flying fists and roaring guns, led the vigilantes into battle with the gang . . .

DOC ADAMS

THE CLAIM-JUMPERS

Complete and Unabridged

LINFORD
Leicester

First published in Great Britain in 2000 by
Robert Hale Limited
London

First Linford Edition
published 2002
by arrangement with
Robert Hale Limited
London

British Library CIP Data

Adams, Doc
The claim-jumpers.—Large print ed.—
Linford western library
1. Western stories
2. Large type books
I. Title
823.9'14 [F]

ISBN 0–7089–9834–8

Published by
F. A. Thorpe (Publishing)
Anstey, Leicestershire

Set by Words & Graphics Ltd.
Anstey, Leicestershire
Printed and bound in Great Britain by
T. J. International Ltd., Padstow, Cornwall

This book is printed on acid-free paper

1

It was evening when the Preacher rode into Jackpot. All the saloons were ablaze with light. Raucous male and female laughter filled the air, mingled with the clink of glasses and the tinny jangle of a honky-tonk piano.

A saloon across the street went suddenly quiet. The Preacher knew what that meant. Sure enough, a moment later the silence was broken by the roar of gunfire.

As the echoes died away, the door of the funeral parlour burst open and a thin man dressed all in black came running out. He had a tall hat in one hand and was trying to button his waistcoat with the other.

'Hey, mister,' he called. 'Where was the shooting at?'

'Hogan's Saloon,' the Preacher replied laconically.

'Thanks.' The mortician turned and ran into the saloon.

Keen businessman, that fella, the Preacher mused to himself. Looks mighty prosperous too. Must be a mort of buryings, hereabouts.

He rode on down the street and came to a halt before a large white house standing all by itself in a corner plot. He swung down from the saddle and tied his horse's reins to the rail, then mounted the steps and knocked on the door.

There was a pause, and then the door opened. A man in a short jacket stood there. He was holding his right hand behind his back.

'This Judge Chaffee's house?'

'It is. Your name, sir?'

'Hunter.'

'Come in, sir. The judge will be pleased to see you.'

The man stepped back to allow Hunter to enter the building. As he did so took his hand from behind his back. It was holding a Starr pocket pistol.

2

The Preacher smiled thinly. 'Expecting trouble?'

'No, sir. Ready for it though.'

The Preacher raised his eyebrows at the sight of the big mahogany table and upholstered furniture that filled the judge's living-room. All this luxury must have been hauled at great expense from St Louis. The judge was clearly a man who liked his comforts and was prepared to pay for them. According to the governor he was also as straight as a die.

There were three men in the room. The Preacher recognized the judge from his description. He had never seen either of the other two before. One of them was as thin as a rail with burning green eyes in a pale face. The other man was fat and jolly.

They saw a tall man, dressed in sombre black broadcloth. His white shirt was tied with a black string tie. His well-worn gunbelt supported a Colt .44 and a Bowie with a nine-inch blade.

'Come in, Mr Hunter,' the judge said warmly. His grip was surprisingly firm for such an old man.

'Let me introduce you to my colleagues.'

He gestured to his left. 'George King, owner of the biggest mine hereabouts, the Lynx.'

The thin man took Hunter's hand gingerly. His fingers felt like a bundle of dry sticks wrapped up in lizardskin.

The fat man didn't wait for the judge to introduce him. He grinned at Hunter and stuck out his hand. 'They call me Jolly Jack Reeve. I own the stageline and one of the general stores.'

'Jolly Jack?' Hunter's eyebrows rose quizzically.

The fat man's chins wobbled with laughter. 'Fits me, don't it.' Then he sobered. 'But I won't be Jolly Jack for much longer if we can't get rid of the Boot Hill Gang. They're ruining my business.'

'*Your* business, Jack?' the other man said tetchily. 'What about mine? You only lose your wagons; I lose my gold!' He pulled a sour face. 'I've had just about enuff of payin' men to hack the damn stuff out of the rock then see those blame outlaws get it!'

The judge held up his pudgy hands. 'Calm down, George. Mr Hunter is here to help us now.'

Muttering crossly to himself the mine-owner slumped into a chair. The other three sat down as well. The judge's servant brought them drinks.

'What do you know about the situation here, Mr Hunter?' the judge asked.

'Only what I've just heard,' the Preacher replied with a smile. 'Someone is robbing your stages, Mr Reeve, and stealing your gold, Mr King.'

'They sure are!' the mine-owner spat furiously.

The judge waved him into silence. 'There have always been badmen and robbers hereabouts, but they were no more than a nuisance until about a year ago. Then they started to get organized under the name of the Boot Hill Gang. By now they number fifty or more — all killers.'

'And they've got Jackpot well and truly treed,' Jolly Jack broke in an aggrieved tone. 'Oh, you *can* get out of town, but not if you're carrying gold. The bastards hold up my stagecoaches and search 'em from top to bottom before they let 'em pass. If they find any gold they take it at gunpoint. Miners who try to sneak it out on their own usually wind up dead.'

'I thought there was a sheriff in Jackpot,' said the Preacher.

'So there is,' replied the judge. 'A man called Burt Ryker. He's pretty good with a gun, too. And he's got a deputy to help him. But it's all they can do to keep the town under control.'

'So they don't even try to fight the Boot Hill Gang,' interjected Jolly Jack.

'That's why us miners got together and set up the vigilantes,' George King said bitterly. 'It worked for a while, then we got word two of the gang was holed up in a cabin up one of the side creeks. They was wanted for killin' a miner and stealin' his poke. But when we got there the birds had flown.' His jaw tightened. 'Someone must have warned 'em we was comin'. Someone in the vigilantes.'

Jolly Jack took over. 'We three trust each other, Mr Hunter, but we don't trust anyone else. We need someone to work under cover, reporting only to us. We know your reputation. We think you are the man for us.'

'There's no preacher in Jackpot right now,' Jolly Jack added slyly, 'so no one will be surprised if you say you've come here to take the post. Maybe people will talk to you, I don't know. But you're our last chance. If this doesn't work we might as well pull up stakes and head out of here, maybe take the other honest citizens with us. Will you take the job?'

'How can I refuse?' Hunter replied. 'The Lord has obviously called me to this place.'

'Good man,' the judge began, then

broke off as the door opened and a young woman came in. She was blonde and beautiful, dressed in a silk dress that rustled when she moved. Her eyes were the clear blue of a mountain lake in spring but the Preacher could clearly see the sadness in them.

'Stacy, this is Mr Hunter,' said the judge. 'Hunter, this is my niece, Stacy Barton. Mrs Barton, that is,' he added hastily.

'Good evening, ma'am,' said Hunter, taking her hand and bowing over it in the courtly style of the old South.

'Good evening, Mr Hunter,' the young woman replied in a voice like the tinkling of silver bells.

'Stacy is looking for her husband,' the judge said quickly. 'He came out here with money to invest in mines, twenty thousand dollars, wasn't it, girl?'

'That's right, Uncle. He wrote me he'd arrived in Jackpot and arranged to buy a likely claim. Then nothing more.'

Hunter felt sorry for the girl. Almost certainly her husband had been robbed and killed. His body would have been stuffed down an abandoned mine shaft and the sides caved in on it. No one had a chance of finding it now.

'Stacy needs to know if he is dead,' the judge explained, 'so that she can probate his will. There is not much money involved, but Stacy needs it.'

'I love my husband, Mr Hunter,' the young woman said softly. 'If he's alive I want to find him; if he's dead I want to bury him properly. Will you help me?'

'Of course, ma'am.'

'Thank you.' The girl smiled warmly at him. 'Then if you'll excuse me, gentlemen.' With a rustle of silk she was gone.

The judge sighed heavily. 'Stacy won't admit it, not even to herself, but Stephen wasn't much good. First there were other women, then he started gambling. When most of their money had gone he got the idea of coming West.

'Maybe he thought he could turn their last twenty thousand into a fortune by speculating in the mining industry. Instead he must have found a lonely grave somewhere out in the hills. If you can find his body she might be able to close that book and maybe even make a new life for herself with someone else.'

'As I said, Judge, I'll do my best,' Hunter said with a touch of grimness in his tone.

'Fair enough. Now I expect you are tired after your ride. Hungry too, I shouldn't wonder. My man is getting a meal ready for you right now.'

The judge's two friends took the hint and made their farewells. The judge's servant showed them out, then returned with a tray on which was a plate of beef and beans and a bottle of beer.

As Hunter tucked into his meal the judge gave him a quick thumb-nail sketch of some of the town's most prominent citizens.

'You can't trust any of 'em though,' the judge said sourly. 'Except Jack and George, that is. Anyone else might be a member of the Boot Hill Gang. Anyone at all.'

'So I should try and remember Psalm eighteen verse eight then?' said the Preacher with a smile.

The judge looked blankly at him.

''It is better to put confidence in the Lord than to trust in any men''

'That's about right,' said the judge grimly. 'You can't trust anyone in Jackpot.'

Hunter changed the subject. 'Where am I going to stay?'

'Here, of course. No one will think it strange if the new preacher lodges with me,' the judge said with a sly chuckle. 'In the morning I'll show you the building our last preacher used as a church.'

Hunter decided to take a walk round the town before turning in for the night. He stalked catfooted along the sidewalks, shooting quick glances into the saloons as he passed by, but not going into any of them. He wasn't looking for trouble just yet.

Hunter recognized some of the men drinking and gambling in the garishly lighted saloons. Their faces were on Wanted posters. Many of their companions wore the same mark of Cain on their vicious, depraved features.

Hunter shook his head thoughtfully. The judge had made his new job sound bad enough, but it seemed he hadn't told him the half of it. Jackpot was chockful of gunmen and killers for hire. This was no place for honest, decent men to try and bring up their families.

Leaving the saloons and bawdy-houses behind him Hunter sauntered down towards the poorer end of town, where the miners lived when they weren't out at the diggings.

Two men came out of an alley ahead of him, strode up to one of the shacks, kicked the door open and pushed their way inside.

A man's angry protest was terminated by the sound of a blow, followed by a heavy crash, as if a body had fallen to the floor of the shack. A woman's scream pierced the night, then the sound was cut off as though one of the men had put his dirty paw over her mouth.

Hunter hadn't meant to show his hand just yet. But he couldn't walk on by and leave these people, whoever they were, to the tender mercies of this pair of thugs. He drew his gun, ran swiftly up to the shack and flattened himself against the rough wooden wall of the building.

The two men had left the plank door wide open. Hunter heard an angry voice snarling, 'Gimme his poke, or it'll be the worse for you!' This brutal speech was followed by the sound of a slap and a woman's muffled scream.

Peering round the doorframe Hunter saw a woman standing in the centre of the room, her eyes wet with tears, her cheek already beginning to discolour from the cruel blow she'd just received. Behind her cowered two small children, a boy of five or so and a girl of three. A man was lying unconscious on the floor at her feet. He was dressed as a miner from the hills.

The men who had knocked the man down were also dressed in miner's duds, but Hunter felt sure they weren't real miners. Their clothes were much too clean for that. Their boots had the high heels of men who spent most of their time in the saddle. Men who did a lot of walking, like miners and farmers, wore flat heels.

One of the men raised his hand to hit the woman again.

'Don't hit me, please!' she cried. 'I don't know where it is. Truly I don't!'

The burlier of the two men laughed nastily. 'Maybe this will change your mind, bitch.' He swung his heavy boot and crashed it into the unconscious man's side.

The woman flew at him, hands curled, and tried to scratch his eyes out. Cursing, he grabbed her round the waist and threw her hard against the wall. The flimsy shack shuddered with the impact. Her two children burst into tears.

Hunter had seen enough. He stepped into the doorway and levelled his gun. 'Freeze, you scum,' he ordered, emphasizing his words by cocking his gun. The metallic click was loud in the sudden silence.

The two men stiffened. They had been caught flat-footed with their backs towards the door. If they tried to turn and draw their guns they'd be dead before they cleared leather, and they knew it.

'What's all this about, ma'am?' asked Hunter.

The woman had fallen to her knees beside the unconscious man and was tenderly mopping the blood from a great cut on his brow with her kerchief.

'Nothing, mister,' she said hastily. She sounded scared. 'My husband here and them two had a difference of opinion, like.'

Hunter raised his eyebrows in disbelief.

The woman flushed. 'That's all it was. Truly, mister!'

Hunter could see that he wasn't

going to learn any more from her. Not while these men were about, anyway. He turned to the two roughnecks. 'Beat it,' he said roughly, jerking his head towards the street.

'I dunno who you think you are, mister,' the shorter, burlier of the two men blustered, 'but you're making a big mistake, buttin' in like this. We got friends in this town.'

'Friends?' Hunter replied contemptuously. 'Rats, more like. Now get going before I forget myself and drill you both where you stand.'

The menace in his voice seemed to get through to the other man, a thin galoot with a drooping moustache. He raised his hands pacifically. 'OK, mister, we're goin',' He pulled at his friend's sleeve'. 'Come on, Jake!'

His partner snarled something under his breath and shrugged him off. 'I'll remember you, stranger,' he grated.

The Preacher smiled thinly. 'See that you do.'

When they had finally gone the

woman looked up from where she was ministering to the man lying on the floor. 'Thank God you came along, mister,' she said fervently. 'They were after my husband's poke. They would have got it but for you.' She began to sob. 'It's all we got left to take with us.'

'Take where?'

'Out of here, of course,' the woman sobbed. We're leavin'.'

'Your man has got a paying claim and you're leaving?' Hunter said in disbelief.

'We got to,' the woman replied bitterly. 'The Boot Hill Gang left their marker on his claim post on Sunday night. A little wooden cross. That means get out before the end of the week or you'll be needing one just like it, only bigger, up on Boot Hill somewhere.'

Hunter was offended to the depths of his soul. How dare they use Christ's cross for their dirty work! In that moment he swore to drive the Boot Hill Gang out of business if it was the last thing he ever did.

'Has this happened before?'

'Lots of times. Anyone who makes a real strike gets told to get out, or be killed. Last week Reuben struck it lucky. Today he sold his claim back to Milton Sawyer, the Land Agent.'

'And got a fair price?' Hunter asked.

''Course not,' the woman said scathingly. 'Sawyer told my Reuben he couldn't give him more'n a few dollars fer it. Said he'd got a pile of claims on his hands and no one to buy 'em.'

'So what did those two want?'

'The little we did get, I guess.' She sighed heavily. 'You frightened them off for now, mister, and we thanks you fer that, but they'll be back, right enough, soon as you've gone. They know we got money, you see, and they wants it. All of it.'

'Well, they won't get it,' Hunter said angrily, and stepped out into the street.

The two would-be robbers hadn't gone far. They were lounging against the side of a building fifty yards down the street. It was clear that they were only waiting for Hunter to leave the area before returning to finish their interrupted business with the unfortunate miner and his family.

Hunter wasn't having that!

'Hey, you!'

'What, us?'

'Yes, you! Drop your guns. I'm taking you down to the sheriff's office.'

The burly gunman hooked his thumbs into his gunbelt and spat derisively. 'We ain't goin' down to the jailhouse just 'cause you say so, mister,' he jeered. 'And don't think that gun'll do yer any good. We know your sort. You wouldn't plug a fella who wasn't holdin' a gun. So how you goin' to make us go with you, eh?'

His companion laughed cynically. 'Wouldn't do you no good, anyways. Ryker wouldn't put us in jail. He knows better than that.'

'Shut up, you fool,' the burly man grated.

'So what?' His partner grinned nastily. 'Who's he gonna tell?' He looked straight into Hunter's cold, grey eyes. 'Come on, mister. Fight us fair or let us go.'

Hunter knew that this was the showdown. He'd tried to take the men in peaceably but he'd failed. If he walked away they would only go back to the miner's shack and rob him and his family of the little they had. He couldn't allow that to happen.

He slid his Colt into its holster and hooked his thumbs into his own wide belt. 'Right,' he said evenly. 'It's your play, gentlemen.'

The two men exchanged glances, then went for their guns. Both men were lightning fast. But Hunter was faster. His Colt .44 was out and blasting a split second before their guns had cleared leather.

Hunter flipped a shot at the taller of the two men, then hurriedly stepped aside as the man's bullet ploughed into the ground at his feet.

The pseudo-miner never got the

chance to trigger another shot. Hunter's bullet entered his right eye and burst its way though the back of his head in a shower of blood and brains. His gun fell from his lifeless fingers as he slumped to the ground.

The other man was a much better shot than his companion, or maybe he had taken an extra split-second to steady his aim. His first shot whipped past the moving Hunter's ear with the sound of an angry bee. But before his finger could tighten on the trigger a second time he took a .44 calibre slug in the chest and went down, coughing blood.

The sound of roaring guns had thrown a sudden pall of silence over the town. Hunter knew that in a moment or two people would be coining lickety-split down the street to see what had happened, more than likely with the eager mortician in the lead.

He ran to the man who had taken a bullet in the chest and kneeled down beside him. The gunman's shirt was drenched in blood. With every laboured breath he took, a froth of bloody bubbles appeared between his lips and ran down over his chin.

'You're dying,' the Preacher said softly. 'I can't do anything about that. No one can. But you still have time to repent your wicked life.'

The stricken man's eyes widened in surprise. The wound in his chest made a sucking sound as he drew in the breath to speak. 'I know you,' he gasped. 'You're the Preach — ' A gush of scarlet blood came from his mouth and he fell back to the sand, dead.

Hunter looked up the street towards the brightly lit centre of town. Men were pouring out of the saloons.

He holstered his pistol and ran off down a nearby alley on cat-like feet.

When the curious crowd reached the scene of the gunfight all there was to be seen was two dead bodies lying in the centre of the street.

By then Hunter was back in the judge's house. As far as he was aware he hadn't been seen by anyone still alive apart from the miner's wife and children, and he knew they wouldn't talk.

The old man was waiting for him. 'What the hell was going on out there?' he asked curiously.

Hunter told him what had happened. 'That woman said her man had been driven off his claim by the Boot Hill Gang.'

'Did she? Well, he's not the only one. The Boot Hill Gang used to rob the miners. Now they're driving them out of town altogether.' The judge stroked his white beard thoughtfully. 'It makes you think someone's trying to take over the whole damned gulch, doesn't it?'

'It certainly seems that way. But who?'

'That's what we want you to find out,' the judge replied with a wry smile.

'Doesn't the sheriff do *anything* to protect the miners?'

'Burt Ryker? He did make a try, right at the beginning. Got a posse together and went out to throw some jumpers off a claim. But the posse was ambushed by the Boot Hill Gang. Three good men were killed and half a dozen more wounded. The next time he tried to raise a posse he couldn't get anyone to join up. So now he doesn't seem to give a damn about the miners. He keeps order in town, after a fashion, and that's about it.

'Not that there's much point in putting men in jail,' the judge added ruefully. 'The honest men in town won't serve on a jury; they're afraid of being beaten up, or worse, so the juries are made up of roughs from the saloons. They always let their friends off. I call myself judge, but it doesn't mean anything. I haven't bossed a proper trial in the last six months.'

His jaw firmed. 'But if you give me the boss man's name I'll round up a jury of men I can trust to convict the bastard if I have to swear 'em in at gunpoint.'

He brought his fist down on to his desk with a crash. 'Then I'll hang him as high as Haman! With him gone we can set about making Jackpot a town worth living in!'

2

The following morning after breakfast,
Judge Chaffee took Hunter to see his
new church. The only thing that
distinguished it from the other buildings in town was the large wooden cross
nailed over the door. They went inside.
Crude wooden benches were ranked
before a simple lectern.

'It's not much,' the judge apologized.

'Do you think God minds?' Hunter
replied with a smile. 'If the people of
Jackpot come to worship Him in this
place He will be satisfied.'

They strolled down the street to the
combined sheriff's office and jail. It
was built of rough stone blocks and
looked solid enough to withstand a
seige. Its windows were heavily
barred. A board outside was plastered
with handbills and Wanted posters.

The judge pushed open the

iron-reinforced door and went in, followed by Hunter.

Burt Ryker was sitting behind his desk with his feet up, smoking a stogie. He was a burly man with a big moustache and clothes that looked a mite too good for his wages. His face showed the marks of a hard life and his eyes were hard. His tall deputy leaned against the wall, a silent witness to everything that went on.

In one of the cells a drunk sat on the bed groaning loudly and holding his head in his hands.

The sheriff greeted the judge with a broad smile that failed to reach his eyes. 'Morning, Judge. Who's your friend?'

'This here's Aaron — '

'Walker!' the preacher said swiftly. Aaron Hunter was a known name in many parts of the West.

'I asked him to come and take poor Hernshaw's place,' the judge said blandly. 'A place like Jackpot needs a powerful lot of preaching, and Mr Walker here is a hell of a preacher.'

Hunter turned and looked at the judge reprovingly.

'I meant a strong preacher, of course,' the judge amended swiftly.

The sheriff tipped his battered hat on to the back of his head and gazed at Hunter with contempt. 'I bet he didn't tell you why the job's vacant right now!'

Hunter decided to play the innocent. 'No, he didn't. Should he have done?'

'Hell, yes!' The sheriff's laugh was not a friendly sound. 'Hernshaw took the notion to preach against drinkin' and gamblin' an' whorin' an such. Waal, the boys didn't take kindly to bein' told off thataway, so one night they grabbed him, stripped off his preacher's duds then tarred and feathered the old fool and ran him out of town on a rail.'

The sheriff's beady eyes glittered derisively. 'Mind the same don't happen to you, Preacher.'

Hunter pretended to look worried. 'Didn't you do anything to try and stop them, Sheriff?'

'Hell, no! They was only havin' a bit of fun. Out here a man gotta fork his own broncs. Parson Hernshaw just wasn't up to it.'

Ryker paused, rolling his cigar from one side of his mouth to the other. 'Are you up to it, Preacher-man?'

'I hope so, I really do,' Hunter said diffidently. His jaw tightened, giving a good imitation of a weak man trying to appear strong. 'Whatever happens, I won't ask *you* for help though.'

'Mind you don't,' the sheriff replied roughly. 'I got no time for Bible-bashers. Now get out of my office. I got work to do.' He tipped his hat to the judge. His deputy didn't even do that much. 'See you around, gents.'

Outside on the sidewalk the judge began to apologize to his guest for the sheriff's rudeness.

Hunter shrugged his shoulders. 'Water off a duck's back!' he said dismissively. 'But I can see why you've got a problem with law and order round here. Why don't you sack him and his closemouthed sidekick and get someone else to do the job?'

'Who'd be fool enough to take it on? And to be fair to the man he's cut the killings way down. When he took the job he let it be known he didn't give a damn about fistfights and drunkenness, but anyone who drew a gun on another man without a real good reason was heading straight for Boot Hill. Made it stick, too. He's pretty slick with a gun. Even the worst killers walk wide of him.'

The judge stroked his beard thoughtfully. 'If anything, he's *too* ready to use his gun. Mind you, none of the men he's killed were any loss to anyone. Rather the reverse.'

They were walking idly down the street when two whiskery miners came out of Jolly Jack Reeve's general store ahead of them and began loading supplies on to a wagon. One of them saw Hunter. His eyes widened. 'Hey, Gandy,' he called, shaking his partner by the shoulder. 'Lookee here, it's — '

'*Walker* is the name,' Hunter said loudly, striding across the street and shaking the man by the hand. Unseen by everyone his hand closed painfully on the other man's work-gnarled fingers. '*Walker*!'

'Right!' the leathery old miner agreed hastily, jerking his mangled fingers from the other man's grip and massaging them with his left hand. 'You remember Preacher *Walker*, Gandy?'

'I sure do,' the man replied, pushing back his broadbrimmed hat and grinning all over his whiskery face. 'Now we'll see some changes around here, I'm thinkin'.'

'You know these men?' the judge enquired, his eyes going from Hunter to the two unshaven miners doubtfully. Would they tell everyone in town who Hunter *really* was and ruin their plan before it had even got started?

'I met these two up on the Silverlode,' Hunter informed him. 'The one with the whiskers is Gandy Dancer. This lean old cuss goes by the name of

Tin-Cup Horton.'

The two miners grinned broadly. 'Seems the Lord's still protectin' you, Preacher,' chuckled Gandy.

'Or maybe the Devil ain't much good at lookin' after his own,' Tin-Cup offered slyly.

'Probably six of one and half a dozen of the other,' Hunter replied with a smile. He turned to Judge Chaffee. 'These are good men, Judge. Reliable. We can trust them.'

The judge clasped hands with each of the miners in turn. If Hunter said they were reliable that was good enough for him.

'You come to help us out 'gainst the Boot Hill Gang?' Gandy Dancer asked hopefully.

'That's right. But don't tell anyone, will you!'

'Hell, no!' Gandy replied with a grin. 'Me and Tin-Cup here know how to keep our mouths shut, don't we, Tin-Cup?'

His partner put his hand over his

mouth and made strangled noises. His wise old eyes twinkled merrily.

'Have you found any gold?' Hunter asked.

'Sure have,' Tin-Cup replied proudly. 'It's the best claim we've had in twenty years of minin'.' His jaw tightened. 'Then we found the Boot Hill Gang's sign on our door. You know what that means? Get out or get shot.'

Gandy took up the tale of woe. 'We was just gettin' supplies fer the journey. Aimin' on movin' out tomorrow or the day after.'

'And now?'

The two grizzled miners exchanged glances. 'Now we ain't fightin' alone,' Gandy responded, 'I guess we'll stick.'

'Good men,' Hunter said approvingly. He turned to Judge Chaffee. 'I think I'll ride out to their claim with them and have a look around. After all, I've got to meet the other miners sometime. This seems as good as any.'

'Just watch yourself, that's all,' the judge replied worriedly. 'Some of those miners up at Jackpot Gulch are pretty rough. They may not take kindly to being visited by a preacher.'

Hunter smiled. 'I'll be careful, Judge.'

When the miners' wagon rolled out of town half an hour later Hunter was riding alongside it. He asked the two miners whether they had been members of the vigilantes.

'Of course we was,' Gandy declared sourly. 'And for a while there we thought we'd got the whole thing licked. Then a fella called Degsy Callahan found the sign of the cross on his claim. Waal, we sat up all night with our guns in our hands. But nothing happened. We did the same for the next two or three nights. More nothing! So we thought it was all a joke and gave it up. Next mornin' we found the poor devil dead at the door of his shack with a damn great knife stickin' in his back.'

'It was allus the same,' Tin-Cup continued bitterly. 'When we tried waitin' for 'em they stayed away. Soon as we gave it up they came back and killed their man the very next night. Some of 'em was shot, others knifed. Now when we hear shootin' we huddle in our shacks and stop up our ears, hopin' they ain't gonna come fer us too.'

'When does the gang usually show up?'

'Between midnight and sun-up.'

'What happens to a claim when the owner has been killed?'

'A bunch of roughnecks shows up next day and takes it over. They don't work it though, just puts up a marker and goes away again. Then someone called Elkington registers the title at the county seat. No one in Jackpot has ever seen him. More'n likely he's a front for the Boot Hill Gang.'

'Best guess is, they want to drive us all out, then take over the whole of Jackpot Gulch,' Gandy said bitterly.

'And bring in machinery?' suggested Hunter.

'That's an idea,' Gandy took off his hat and scratched his bald patch thoughtfully. 'Maybe they could try this newfangled hydraulic mining if they had the whole damn creek to themselves.'

'But it'd cost a fortune,' Tin-Cup protested.

'Yeah. You're lookin' for a man with plenty of cash behind him.'

'Someone like George King of the Lynx?' Hunter offered delicately.

'Naw,' Gandy shook his head. 'He's a good man, George. When the Boot Hill Gang tried to drive him off the Lynx he armed his workers and stood a siege for three days. Killed more'n a few of the bastards. They leave him alone now.'

It took more than two hours to reach the deeply rutted track that led into the steep-sided gulch where most of the mines were situated. Hunter thought it looked like one of the byways of Hell. The rugged hillsides were pierced with the mouths of the mineshafts. Each claim was marked off from its neighbours by wooden posts. Tin nameplates, punched with the miner's name or mark had been nailed to the posts.

Heaps of rock torn from the interior of the mountain and stripped of its ore lay on either side of the trail. The thump of hammers filled the air as miners, stripped to the waist, broke up the larger lumps of rock and then mashed them into gravel. Only the bigger mines could afford mechanical ore crushers.

The stream that had once run sparkling down from the mountain was thick with mud and sewage and stank abominably. Every few yards leats led off to wooden rockerboxes where hopeful miners washed the crushed ore and picked through the refuse in the bottom of the pans for specks of gold. The miners themselves were filthy and unshaven. Their shacks were crude hovels surrounded by piles of rusty tins. Few of them had bothered to dig proper latrines and clouds of fat black flies buzzed everywhere.

Hunter reminded himself that at least

these men were prepared to work hard and honestly for their riches. The town of Jackpot was full of men who were prepared to dip their hands in blood in order to get rich.

As the wagon with Hunter riding beside it came lurching up the track, the miners stopped working on their claims to watch it pass by. They greeted Gandy and Tin-Cup in friendly fashion but stared curiously at the black-clad figure of the stranger.

Then a burly miner strode into the centre of the track and raised a work-gnarled hand. The wagon halted.

'Who's the dude, Gandy?' the miner said scornfully.

'This here's Preacher Walker,' Gandy Dancer replied evenly, though a smile was lurking behind his bushy moustache. The burly miner in front of him was going to get an unpleasant surprise. That was OK by him. He didn't like Dutch Bronson anyway. The man was much too inclined to throw his weight about.

'Turn that hoss around and ride straight out of here, Mister Preacherman,' sneered Bronson. We ain't got use for Bible bashers in Jackpot Gulch.'

'I disagree,' Hunter replied cheerfully. 'If your soul is half as mucky as your body you need to be washed in the blood of the Lamb even more than you need to be washed in the waters of the river.'

The miners laughed and slapped their thighs. 'Got you there, Kurt!' yelled one.

Bronson gave a roar of anger. 'Get down off that hoss, mister, and say that again.'

Hunter swung down from the saddle and shrugged out of his coat, handing it to Gandy to hold. The other miners pressed forward eagerly to see the fun. None of them expected the stranger to last long against Bronson. But watching a fight made a change from swinging a pick or standing up to your knees in icy water panning for gold.

Bronson came forward, fists swinging. Hunter sidestepped his clumsy rush and clipped him on the ear as he went by. The huge miner roared like an angry bull and swung round, but before he could get set Hunter danced in, planted a left and a right in his fleshy face and swung away.

Bronson lost his temper. He was used to standing toe to toe with his opponents, slugging it out until the man with the heaviest fists won the match. But Hunter knew that the best way to deal with a slugger like Bronson was to keep out of his reach and cut him up at leisure.

The miner swung a heavy fist at Hunter's head. The Preacher ducked and the force of the blow almost swung Bronson off his feet. Hunter chopped a fist into Bronson's face and slid away, leaving the miner standing flatfooted and looking mighty foolish.

'Fight him, man. Don't tickle him,' the crowd exhorted the Preacher. But Hunter was in no mood to oblige. He didn't want to return to town all cut and bleeding. It was the wrong image for a preacher. He wanted to end this fight without getting hurt too obviously.

Bronson lurched forward again, fists swinging, Hunter stepped inside the flailing arms and drove a left and a right to the big man's belly. Bronson whoofed as the breath left him but recovered quickly enough to swing his iron-shod boot at Hunter's crotch.

Quick as lightning Hunter grasped the boot and upended Bronson. The big man crashed on to his back in the mud and lay there dazed, all the breath driven out of his body.

'Had enough?' Hunter asked, and put out a hand to help the big man to his feet.

Bronson smiled evilly, grasped the outstretched hand and surged to his feet. His bullet head struck Hunter in the midriff.

Now it was Hunter's turn to gasp as the breath left his lungs in an explosive puff. He staggered back, but Bronson still held on to his hand and jerked him closer. The big man's fist crashed into Hunter's chin with the force of a piledriver.

The Preacher staggered and went down.

Bronson gave a cry of triumph. Stepping forward he swung his heavy boot into Hunter's side. Hunter rolled away, partially breaking the force of the blow. Bronson came after him. This was his chance to stomp the preacher-man into the dirt.

But Hunter was ready for him. He grasped the swinging foot and upended Bronson again. The big man went down like a falling tree. Hunter scrambled to his feet and waited while Bronson got up.

Both men were showing the effects of their rough and tumble. Their clothes were smeared with mud. Bronson's face was a mask of blood where Hunter's gloved hands had cut and sliced at his fleshy features. Hunter was favouring his left side where the big miner's boots had caught him. But both men were still full of fight.

The crowd egged them on with shouts of 'Smash him, Bronson', and 'Go it, Preacher-man!' They seemed not to care which man won the fight. They were enjoying it too much for that.

But Hunter had had enough of pussyfooting around. As Bronson came towards him, fists swinging, he stepped inside the big man's reach and pounded his solar plexus with a flurry of blows, tucking his head into his opponent's chest where Bronson could not get at him.

Bronson hammered on Hunter's kidneys with his iron-hard fists until the preacher thought he would break in half. Then Bronson brought up his knee. Hunter turned and took it on the thigh.

Bronson shoved Hunter away and staggered backwards, breathing heavily. His belly was on fire. It felt as though he had been kicked by a mule.

Hunter tottered after him. He knew

he had to end the fight soon or he would collapse. The big man could hit too hard. He summoned all his strength and brought up his fist from somewhere near his knees, with all the force in his battered body. It impacted on Bronson's bristly chin with the force of a triphammer. Bronson's eyes glazed, he swayed from side to side and then fell like a tree face down into the dirt.

Hunter had won.

The miners gave him a ragged cheer. Bronson was far from popular amongst them.

Tin-Cup handed Hunter a canteen full of water. Hunter took a swig, spat it out, then up-ended the canteen over his head, using a handkerchief from his pants pocket to wipe the blood from his face.

Bronson struggled to his feet and staggered away. Reaching his hut he went inside and slammed the door.

'Anyone else object to my preaching around here?' Hunter said to the admiring crowd of miners.

One of the men stepped forward. 'No, *sir*. If'n you punch that Bible the way you punched Bronson just now we'll be mighty glad to hear you do it.'

Hunter couln't help smiling at them despite the pain of his split and bleeding lips. 'I'll do my best, boys,' he said. 'With the help of the Lord. First though, we'll have a hymn.'

His strong baritone led off with that old favourite, 'Rock of Ages, cleft for me . . . '

The miners joined in one by one until the rocky walls of the gulch echoed and re-echoed to the sound of their voices.

Then Hunter began to preach. He took as his text Job chapter 36 verse 19: 'Will He esteem thy riches? No, not gold, nor all the forces of strength', and preached a powerful sermon against the lust for gold which was driving the miners to ruin this beautiful countryside and the Boot Hill Gang to murder and rob the miners.

Some of the men eyed him askance,

but others were clearly taking the message to heart. Then Hunter announced another hymn.

At the end of the short service, Hunter invited the miners and their families to come to meeting in town on Sunday next, then mounted his horse and trotted off down the trail to town.

The miners stood and watched him out of sight, then returned to their claims and started work.

★   ★   ★

Gandy flicked the reins; his mule leaned against the collar and the wagon creaked into movement. The two men's claim was way up one of the side valleys. The track that led to it was rocky and steep and it took them some time to get there.

When they arrived, Tin-Cup unhitched their mule and unloaded the wagon while Gandy cooked up a mess of bacon and beans. A short while later Hunter rode up, having circled through the hills and got to their claim without being seen by any of the other miners. He joined the two at their simple meal.

When night came and the lights in the miners' huts began to go out one by one, Hunter unpacked his gunbelt from his saddle-bag and strapped it round his waist. Then the three men left their hut and took up their positions behind some large rocks on the hillside.

They waited for what seemed like a very long time. The night was cold and they were beginning to wonder whether they had made a mistake when they heard the clink of iron horseshoes on the rocky track. A band of riders was approaching the mine. They had come over the hills and down into the creek from the north. That way they avoided passing any other claim. They aimed to kill Gandy and Tin-Cup and make their getaway before any of the other miners could come to help the two crusty old coots.

That was their plan, anyway.

Soon the oncoming riders were

visible as darker shapes against the rocks. There were eight of them altogether. A man in a wide-brimmed hat was in the lead.

When they got to within a hundred yards or so of the hut, they dismounted and ground-hobbled their horses. Then they split up. Three men picked their way down the slope towards the shelter of the sluices and rockers by the stream, rested the barrels of their rifles on the woodwork, and took aim at the door of the hut. Another three men took up their positions by the mouth of the mineshaft.

The man with the wide-brimmed hat drew his pistol and made straight for the hut, followed by the remaining gunman. He knocked softly on the door. There was no reply.

The boss-man laughed harshly. 'Seems like they seen sense, boys,' he called softly. He opened the door by pulling the latch string, and peered inside. The hut was quite empty.

'Come on boys,' he called.

The other men left their positions and came to join him, their guns swinging idly from their hands.

Hunter waited until they were all bunched up in front of the hut before calling out, 'Drop your guns. We've got you covered.'

The men whirled round, hastily swinging up their guns to the ready position. But they had nothing to aim at. The night was as dark as the inside of a coffin.

'I mean it,' Hunter repeated urgently. 'Drop 'em or die!'

The reply that came was utterly unexpected. 'I know that voice!' one of the gunmen called excitedly. 'It's the new preacher! He was talking to the judge in town this morning. What the hell's he doing out here?'

Hunter went cold inside. He had hoped to take at least one of these men alive. Now they would all have to die in order to preserve his secret.

'I dunno. I don't care neither!' the man with the wide-brimmed hat said roughly. 'Kill him with the others!' He threw himself to the ground and triggered a shot in the direction from which he thought Hunter's voice had come. The slug whined high over the Preacher's head.

Gandy Dancer swung the muzzle of his old Springfield rifle towards the gunflash. His finger tightened on the trigger. A tongue of flame lit up the night. There was a scream from the darkness across the way as the spinning lump of lead hit its mark.

The remaining gunmen fired back, and for the next few minutes the night was torn by muzzle flames, the crash of gunfire and the whine of ricocheting bullets.

But while Hunter and his friends were hunkered down behind some large rocks, the members of the Boot Hill Gang had been caught out in the open. There was just enough light for their shapes to be seen against the dark hillside.

Hunter flipped two bullets into the

man with the wide-brimmed hat, who went to his knees, then fell on to his side. His sidekick fired wildly into the darkness. Hunter levelled his gun and shot him through the heart.

Tin-Cup pulled both triggers of his shotgun at once. The double cloud of shot blasted another two men to doll-rags.

From the sound of his groans, Gandy's victim had been hit hard. But he was still full of fight. His gun barked again and again. His third shot struck splinters from the rock beside the whiskery old miner. That was much too close for comfort.

But Gandy had been biding his time while he reloaded his single-shot weapon. Now he drew a bead on a spot a foot to the right of the tongue of flame from his enemy's gun and squeezed the trigger gently. Hit clean through the heart, the gunman fell back, stone dead.

The deaths of their companions had driven the fight out of the other three men. They turned and ran towards their horses.

But Hunter couldn't let them get away. For his own safety all eight gunmen had to die.

Consoling himself with the thought that these men were undoubtedly long overdue for death he rested his pistol over his left forearm and drew a bead on the nearest of them. His pistol cracked and the man threw up his arms and fell forward into the little stream. A split second later Gandy's old rifle barked and another man fell in a heap.

The last man jinked desperately from side to side as he ran. Hunter took careful aim and sent a bullet into the back of his skull. The gunman dropped like a puppet whose strings had been cut.

As if that had been some sort of signal the edge of the moon began to show over the crest of the nearby ridge, casting a faint, wan light on the scene of carnage in the little valley. Eight men were dead or dying. Pools of spilt blood showed black against the grey rocks.

The men from the Boot Hill Gang hadn't been expecting to meet this sort of opposition. They had been careless and had paid for it with their lives.

Down the valley, lights were going on in the miners' rough cabins. The crash of gunfire had woken everyone up. But no one came to investigate. They probably thought that Gandy and Tin-Cup had been killed by the Boot Hill Gang. They would find out differently in the morning.

Under Hunter's direction the two miners hauled the bodies to one side of the trail and left them there in a row as a warning to any of their friends who happened by.

As always after a killing Hunter felt a tide of sadness come stealing over him. If these men had lived they *might* have changed their wicked ways and turned into model citizens. But now they would never have the chance. Death put an end to choices, at least as far as *this* world was concerned.

Gandy and Tin-Cup were delighted by the success of their ambush. 'That's showed 'em!' gloated Tin-Cup. 'They won't come this way again in a hurry!'

'Oh yes they will!' Hunter said warningly. 'They'll have to kill you now, or they might as well give up altogether. And I can't be with you all the time. I've got other fish to fry.'

'But what do we do now?' Gandy said worriedly. 'We can't work our claim if we're always lookin' over our shoulders for gunmen.'

'There are a number of men in town who've been warned off their claims. I'll send them up to join you. We can be sure they are not in the gang.'

'I guess not,' Tin-Cup agreed with a shrug.

'Next time you hear that someone has been given notice to quit take all the men I've sent you and lay an ambush by his cabin on the following night. A few more massacres like this and the Boot Hill Gang will start to break up.'

Gandy rubbed his chin thoughtfully. 'I can see the sense in what you're sayin', Preacher, but I sure hate to stop workin' my claim now it's looking good.'

'Stop grousin', you old fool,' Tin-Cup said with a grin. 'You're still alive, ain't yer? If it weren't fer the Preacher here you'd be lookin' at flowers from the wrong side, I'm thinkin'.'

Gandy Dancer looked sheepishly at the tall figure of the Preacher. 'I guess this ornery old cuss has got the right of it after all. I'll do as he says.'

'Good man!' Hunter walked over to his horse and swung into the saddle.

'Where are you off to now?'

'Back to town, of course. We can't have anyone suspecting a preacher of being tied up with the vigilantes, can we?'

Gandy gave a chuckle. 'I guess not. When shall we see you again?'

'I can't say. If you need to contact me, leave a message with the judge.'

Leaving the two miners standing

beside the bodies of the eight dead gunmen, Hunter dug his heels into his horse's sides and trotted up into the hills. He had a long ride ahead of him, but with God's help he would get back to town without being seen by anyone.

3

Later that morning Hunter was walking down the main street when he was accosted by the burly figure of Sheriff Ryker.

'I got a job for you, Preacher' he said with a satirical curl of the lip.

'Oh yes?' Hunter enquired blandly.

'A buryin'. Ten of 'em.'

Hunter pretended to look shocked. 'Ten men dead! What kind of town is this?'

'Oh, they didn't all happen here,' Ryker said a mite defensively. 'Eight of 'em was shot out at the diggin's. On Gandy and Tin-Cup's claim.' The sheriff glowered at Hunter. 'Say ... didn't I see you talking to those two old coots yesterday?'

'That's right. Apparently the Boot Hill Gang had warned them to get out or be killed. They were asking me if I thought they ought to pull up stakes and hightail it out of here, or stick it out and risk being shot.'

The sheriff's eyes bored into the Preacher's. 'And what did you tell 'em?'

Hunter spread his hands. 'That gold is never worth dying for, of course. As we read in the Gospel of Matthew chapter six verse nineteen: 'Lay not up for yourselves treasure on earth . . . '.'

'I guess you can find anythin' in the Bible if you know where to look,' the sheriff interrupted him scornfully. 'But it was good advice, all the same. Did they say they was goin'ter take it?'

'Yes, they did. They were aiming to get out before nightfall.' The Preacher eyed the sheriff thoughtfully. 'Why all the questions, Sheriff?'

Ryker grunted sourly. 'Because I wondered if they was the ones did the killin'. But it ain't likely. Two old men like that ain't about ter shoot down eight gunmen and get off scot free themselves.'

'I wouldn't have thought so either,' agreed Hunter.

The sheriff pointed up the street towards the distant graveyard on the hill. 'That's yer first job, Preacher. Them fellers' bodies are up there already. Their graves have been dug too.'

Hunter stroked his chin thoughtfully. Why did Ryker want the dead men buried so soon? It was usual to put them on public display for a while as a warning to others.

Ryker mistook the reason for his hesitation. 'Don't worry, Preacher,' he said contemptuously. 'You'll get paid.'

'How much?' demanded Hunter. If he could get a reputation for veniality it would help to disarm suspicion.

The sheriff eyed him scornfully. So the new preacher was greedy for gold, was he? Then he wouldn't give the Boot Hill Gang any problems. Jackpot's last preacher had spoken out against the Boot Hill Gang. That was the real reason he'd been run out of town on a rail.

'Five dollars a body. That suit you?'

The Preacher rubbed his hands together as though he could already feel the gold pieces sifting through his fingers. 'It's generous, Sheriff. Mighty generous.'

'Don't thank me,' the sheriff growled. 'The town council sets the fee. I think it's a waste of money, myself.'

Hunter pretended to be shocked. 'Aren't you a believing man, Sheriff?'

'Hell, no! I don't want no preacher mouthing empty words over me when my time comes, and I don't see why anyone else does either,' the sheriff said fiercely. 'What do I care what happens to my corpse after I'm dead? I won't be there to watch, will I?'

The Preacher shook his head sadly. 'You are a Godless man, Sheriff. But I shall pray for you, none the less.'

Ryker went red with anger. 'Do what you like,' he snapped. 'I ain't stoppin' you.' He turned on his heel and stalked off without another word.

As Hunter walked up the street

towards the graveyard a number of men came out of the Golden Ball saloon and fell in behind him. They were much more flashily dressed than the average cowhand or miner. Most of them looked as if they had never done a good day's work in their lives, let alone grubbed in the dirt for gold. Hunter guessed they were probably members of the Boot Hill Gang. But how to prove it?

When he got to the cemetery he found a crowd of men already there. Rough and unshaven, looking as though they hadn't had a bath in weeks, they were clearly miners. Hunter recognized some of them from yesterday. Many of them had bottles of whiskey in their hands. Some of them were already half drunk. They had obviously come to celebrate the deaths of the men who had terrorized them for so long.

When the miners saw the gang of men coming up the hill behind Hunter they sobered rapidly. The newcomers were hung about with guns and looked as if they knew how to use them.

Most of the miners had brought some kind of weapon with them to the burying. In moments the graveyard was loud with the sound of guns being cocked.

The gunmen spread out in a long line facing the miners across the eight open graves. Their faces were hard. Their hands hovered over their guns. Most of them were longing for an excuse to pull their guns and start blasting.

One of them elected himself spokesman. He gestured towards the row of bodies lying on the dusty earth. 'These men was our friends, Preacher,' he grated. 'Give them a good send off, or you'll regret it!'

An angry growl arose from the group of miners. Then the battered figure of Dutch Bronson stepped forward. He held an old shotgun in his meaty hands. He glared at Hunter. 'Don't waste yer breath on *them*, Preacher,' he said scathingly. 'They was scum, an' better off dead. More'n likely they're burnin' in Hell already. Shovel 'em underground without any more bleatin' an' let's all go home.'

Hunter stepped forward. His black-clad figure dominated the scene. 'Never say that!' he said with authority. 'If they were sinners they are paying for it now. It is for God to judge them, not us fallible men.'

'Someone sure judged 'em! With a six-gun!' one of the miners shouted derisively. The other miners burst out laughing. The gunmen scowled and tightened their grip on their gunbutts.

Hunter knew that the situation was perched on a knife-edge. One more remark like that and guns would start roaring across the open graves.

'The dead should always be treated with respect,' he said sharply, 'whatever they did in life. If you men don't know how to behave at a funeral I suggest you leave. Right now!'

The miners shuffled their feet and exchanged embarrassed glances. First one man sidled away, then another and another. Hunter waited silently, with folded arms, until they had all gone. Only the bullyboys of the Boot Hill Gang were left at the graveside.

Hunter turned to face them. 'Now, gentlemen,' he said calmly. 'Let us proceed with the burying.'

They stood in silence while Hunter read the burial service over the eight dead gunmen. When it was over they all walked back to town together.

One of the men said to Hunter: 'You shape like a real man, Preacher. You could do better than Bible-bashin'. Come in with us and you could get rich.'

'Doing what? Mining?' Hunter said quizzically, looking them up and down. Their clothes were far too good for working miners.

'Yeah, mining,' one of the other men said drily. His companions snickered loudly.

The man who had spoken first glared at them until they fell silent again. 'You ain't no friend to them dirty mudrats,

Preacher! You just showed us that! So why not join us, eh?'

Hunter turned on him sharply. 'I was only doing my duty. Those men weren't proper mourners. They had come to gloat over the bodies. I won't have that. Every man deserves dignity in death, whatever he was in life. If I'd been burying a miner and you men had turned up to gloat I would have done the same.' He smiled slyly. 'A man in my position can't be seen to take sides, you see.'

The gunman closed one eye in a meaningful wink. He thought he knew what the Preacher was trying to tell him. His boss would be interested too.

Back in town Hunter was stopped by Sheriff Ryker. He was jingling a handful of gold eagles in his hand. 'Here's your pay, Preacher,' he sneered. 'Easy money, ain't it?'

Hunter took the coins and slipped them into his pocket. 'The labourer is worthy of his hire, Sheriff,' he said sanctimoniously.

Sheriff Ryker was a bad man, but no hypocrite, and Hunter's oily tone offended him. He pursed his lips and spat. The spittle landed within an inch of Hunter's boot.

Hunter studiously ignored the insult. 'I did my poor best to bring some comfort to those unfortunate men's friends,' he said piously. 'Now I have some calls to make in the town. If you'll excuse me?'

The sheriff snorted with disgust. Anyone who listened to this oily apology for a man of God was a fool, or worse. He strode away without a word.

Hunter congratulated himself on having pulled the wool over the sheriff's eyes. While Ryker thought him a money-grubbing hypocrite he would never suspect him of being the driving forge behind the revived vigilante organization.

But maybe Ryker wasn't in cahoots with the Boot Hill Gang after all. Maybe, as the judge had suggested, he had merely given up hope of beating the robbers and was content to keep the town under control. Only time would tell.

Hunter decided to go and see the woman he had helped the night before. As he approached the shack he saw the curtain over the window quiver. Then the woman opened the door. Her face was white and drawn.

'How is your husband today?' Hunter began.

'He's gone!' she blurted.

'Gone! Gone where?'

The woman hesitated, then said in a rush, 'I know I can trust you, after what you did last night. My man's gone up into the hills.'

Hunter raised his eyebrows. Things were happening already.

'Did he go alone?' he asked casually.

The woman shook her head. 'Some friends of his, miners, came and talked to him. He wouldn't tell me what they said, but he took his gun and bedroll and went with them.'

'Was one of the miners a whiskery

old coot with a finger missing from his right hand, and another a tall thin galoot with a red neckerchief?'

The woman was surprised, then suspicious. 'That's right. Do you know them?'

Hunter smiled reassuringly. 'I do. And I know where he's gone. He's joined some men who have decided to fight back against the Boot Hill Gang.'

The woman was dismayed. 'My Reuben's no gunfighter,' she wailed. 'He'll be killed! Why couldn't he have agreed to leave town peacefully, like I wanted?'

'He wouldn't be much of a man if he'd done that, would he?' Hunter said gravely. 'And it would be just the same in the next town and the next. Once you start running you can never stop. Take it from me, Mrs . . . ?'

'Wilson,' the woman replied automatically.

'Your man is doing the right thing. God will protect him, I promise you.'

'How I wish I could believe that,' the

woman said tearfully, her hands twisting and turning in the folds of her apron.

'Believe it!' Hunter said firmly. 'Now go back inside your house and wait. The fightback has begun. Soon the Boot Hill Gang will be beaten. Then Jackpot will become a fine place to live and bring up your children.'

Hunter went back to the judge's house for lunch. The two men were joined by Stacy Barton. As she took her seat at the table Hunter was struck once more by her beauty. In some ways she reminded him of his own wife, who had been killed in the dying days of the War Between the States. He felt a surge of protective feeling towards her. If he could help her in any way, he would.

As he had expected, her first words were of her husband.

'Have you any news of Stephen, Mr Hunter?' she said hopefully.

'Not yet. But I have put the word out with the miners. If he's anywhere up at the diggings, they'll let me know. But you must realize the chances are that he's dead.'

'He's *not* dead!' There was utter conviction in her voice. 'I would know if he were. He is alive.'

'Then maybe he has lost his memory.'

'That was my own thought, Mr Hunter.'

'Have you got a photograph of him?'

'Yes. I'll get it.' She left the room and returned a few minutes later with a piece of pasteboard.

Hunter examined it closely. The man was handsome enough, but his chin was weak and his eyes had a shifty look. He could see why the judge had said that Stephen Barton was no good.

'May I keep this?' he said. 'To show around?'

'Of course you may. I can see Stephen plain in my mind's eye,' she replied with a funny little smile. 'What good is a piece of pasteboard to me?'

After lunch Hunter went back down to the town. He called in on Milton

70

Sawyer, the claims agent. The man was fat and prosperous-looking in a tailored suit and fancy waistcoat. He was sitting at his desk smoking a big cigar, which he used to wave the Preacher to a seat.

'Why hello, Preacher,' he said effusively. 'Want to buy a claim?'

'Why? Have you got some to sell?'

Milton Sawyer reached into the drawer of his desk and pulled out a thin bundle of documents. 'Just a few.'

The Preacher raised his eyebrows. 'The judge told me the miners are too scared of the Boot Hill Gang to even think of selling. That they just abandon their claims and leave the area.'

'He's right. Most of them do. But if they've got the guts to come to me I try to give them enough for a road stake at least. After all, I'm partly responsible for bringing them here!'

'That's a very Christian attitude, my dear sir,' the Preacher said approvingly, 'but what do you mean, you brought them here?'

'You know how this place got started?'

The Preacher kept his face blank. 'Tell me.'

'A lone prospector found gold in the creek. Not much, but enough to pay for a few drinks. There was no town here then, of course. So he went to the nearest place with a saloon, that's Elkhorn, thirty miles away.'

He took a deep draw on his cigar. 'Well, I was in the saloon and heard him boasting about finding gold here. Then he got into a fight and was killed. I lit out of there like someone had shoved a burr under my tail and rode lickety-split to the county seat.'

He gave the Preacher an embarrassed smile. 'I guessed he hadn't yet filed on the land, you see. And I was right. So I ended up owning the whole gulch.'

The Preacher's eyes shot up. If that was true Sawyer ought to be a very rich man indeed. But his office was small and although he looked prosperous enough he gave no sign of possessing great wealth. He didn't have to wait long for the explanation.

'I sold the land off in chunks,' Sawyer went on. 'I didn't believe he'd made a big strike, thought it was just a flash in the pan. Then men started striking it rich.' He grinned ruefully. 'I *did* feel sick. So if anyone comes to me wanting to sell I'm more'n willing to buy 'em back again.'

Hunter rubbed his chin thoughtfully. This story didn't show Sawyer in a very good light, did it? Then he had second thoughts. Maybe by admitting to greed and duplicity the land agent hoped to avoid being accused of working hand in glove with the Boot Hill Gang.

Maybe Sawyer had been able to hear his thoughts. 'I guess you're wondering why I'm telling you all this,' he said with an embarrassed laugh.

The Preacher nodded.

'It's simple enough, Mr Walker: I know I'm not really cheating anyone, but I still don't feel entirely easy in my mind, all the same. I been wanting to tell someone about it, and a preacher is like a priest, can't tell anyone what he hears, ain't that right?'

'Not exactly,' the Preacher replied. 'But your secret is safe with me.'

The agent let out his breath in a sigh of relief 'Thank God for that.' Then his manner changed, becoming business-like again. 'Now, are you quite sure you don't want to buy a claim?'

'No, thanks,' the Preacher replied with a smile. 'But you can do something for me.' He took the picture of Stephen Barton from his pocket and showed it to Sawyer. 'Have you seen this man anywhere?'

Sawyer examined it briefly and handed it back. 'No. Should I have done?'

The Preacher shrugged dismissively. 'It doesn't matter.' Making his farewells he left Sawyer's office.

Hunter spent the next couple of hours acquainting himself with the town and its people. He went into every shop and business and introduced himself to the proprietor and his family. He invited them all to come to meeting on the following Sunday.

Then he went round all the cabins and shacks which housed the miners' families. Here the signs of poverty were more obvious.

Some of the miners' womenfolk turned him away with a curse or a sneer, but most of them promised to come to the service on Sunday and bring their children with them.

Hunter had no illusions about their motives for agreeing to come to meeting. It was the sing-song they were looking forward to, not the opportunity of hearing him preach. But all he could do was scatter the seed as widely as he could: God would ensure that not all of it fell on stony ground.

He was just going back to the judge's house for dinner when a pair of lathered horses came into town pulling a heavy wagon. As he watched with interest they thundered down Main

Street and pulled up in a cloud of dust in front of the sheriff's office.

The man at the reins was nursing a wounded arm. The guard's body lolled on the bench beside him. Three more men were lying on the flatbed. Two of them were already dead and one was plainly in a bad way and like to die.

A crowd quickly gathered round the wagon. Some of the men helped the driver off the box and sat him down in a rocker on the stoop. Another went running for the doctor.

Hearing the commotion Sheriff Ryker and his deputy rushed out of their office. 'What happened to you, Wally?' the sheriff asked the wounded man.

'The Boot Hill Gang,' the man replied bitterly. 'We didn't have a chance, Sheriff. There was ten of 'em, hiding in the rocks beside the trail less'n a mile from the Lynx. Opened up on us without any warning, they did. Bill here was the first to get it, then the others; I was lucky, I guess, I only got this!' He held up his wounded arm. 'They must have wanted someone to drive the wagon into town afterwards. They took the gold, all of it, then skedaddled into the hills. I loaded the bodies on to the flatbed and lit out for town.'

Doctor Sandilands came running up, bag in hand. By then the wounded man on the flatbed had died. He examined the driver's wound. 'You're a lucky man, Wally,' he declared jovially. 'The bullet went right through without hitting the bone. You'll be using that arm again in no time.' He ordered him to be taken into the hotel and put to bed.

Ebenezer Widdowson, the mortician, was hovering on the edge of the crowd like a hungry vulture. Sheriff Ryker caught his eye. 'OK, Ebenezer. Take 'em away. They're all yours!'

'Thank you, Sheriff,' the mortician said obsequiously. He hopped up on to the buckboard. The horses had been waiting patiently, heads down. Now their heads came up as he seized the reins.

But before Widdowson could urge the horses into motion George King came pushing through the crowd. He took one glance at the piled bodies in the wagon and turned first red, then white with fury.

'The Boot Hill Gang do this?' he spat at Sheriff Ryker.

'I guess so,' the man with the badge replied levelly. 'Wally thought so, anyway.'

'Where is he?'

'Over at the hotel. He caught a bullet in the arm. Nothing serious though.'

'Thank God for that.' The mine-owner's green eyes blazed balefully at the burly sheriff. 'But they still killed three of my men and stole my gold. What are you gonna do about it, Sheriff?'

'Yeah! What about it, Ryker!' yelled someone at the back of the crowd. Other men took up the cry. They were townsmen and miners mostly. The flashily dressed men from the saloons exchanged knowing glances but held their tongues.

Ryker scowled at George King. The mine-owner was the richest man in the county. It made sense to try and keep him sweet. But the sheriff had good reasons for not wanting to lead a posse into the hills.

'All right! All right!' he bawled. 'Give a man a chance to speak!'

The yelling slowly died away.

'You all know what happened last time we rode out to chase those murdering devils,' he said sourly. 'We was ambushed and shot to doll-rags. But if you men want to try again, I'm game.' His cynical eyes moved from face to face. 'How about you, Cassidy? Or you, Tompkins? Watts will volunteer, won't you Watts? You're not scared, are you, Snell? Bauer will come with us, I'm sure. And Hitchin too!'

The men he had named flushed bright red but made no reply. Their enthusiasm for the fight had suddenly evaporated. On the edges of the crowd men who had been full of belligerence a moment before began to sidle away.

Ryker took a cigar from his top pocket and stuck it between his fleshy lips. He struck a match on the seat of his jeans and lit it, then blew a cloud of pungent smoke into the faces of the men at the front of the crowd. 'You won't fight?' he said contemptuously. 'Then go home.'

He spat in the dust, then turned on his heel and stumped off down the street to the jail, went inside and slammed the door.

Ebenezer Widdowson flicked the reins and the two tired horses leaned wearily into their collars once more and the wagon and its bloody freight rolled off down the street.

Sick to his stomach, George King watched the death cart roll away and the ashamed townspeople disperse to their homes. Would no one avenge his murdered employees? And find his missing gold?

He had to blame someone, and Deputy Zachary Burns was the only one handy. He grabbed the young man's shoulder and pulled the taciturn deputy round to face him. 'A fine pair of lawmen you are!' he sneered. 'More than likely you're both in cahoots with the Boot Hill Gang!'

By now all the solid citizens and unemployed miners had sidled away. Only a few of the flashily dressed loafers from the saloons were left to hear this insulting remark.

Burns twisted out of the mine-owner's grasp and took a couple of steps backwards. 'I'll kill you for that,' he snarled.

George King went white. He was wearing a gun, everyone did, but he was no gunman. Burns would kill him, sure as shooting. He raised his hands placatingly. 'I'm sorry, Zack,' he stammered. 'I didn't mean it.'

Burns knew it. But he meant to kill the mine-owner all the same. He could rely on the watching men to back up his story.

'You said it, King. Now prove it,' he said coldly. 'Draw!'

George King realized that he had come to the end of his rope. For some reason Zachary Burns was determined to kill him. But he was no coward. If he was going to die he would go down shooting. He flipped back the skirt of his coat to expose the handle of his pistol.

Burns tensed, his hand hovering over his gunbutt.

Suddenly the black-clad figure of the Preacher thrust between the two men.

'Stop!' he said in commanding tones. 'Do not break the sixth commandment! Man should not kill his fellow man!'

For a moment Burns was taken aback. The preacher's sonorous voice held all the authority of an Old Testament prophet. But he wasn't the man to be daunted for long. As for the Ten Commandments, he had broken them all in his time, most of them more than once.

'Out of the way, Preacher-man,' he grated. 'Or I'll kill you too.'

The Preacher smiled thinly. 'No, you won't.' He grasped the lapels of his frock coat and opened it wide. Everyone could see that he wasn't wearing a gun. 'You wouldn't shoot an unarmed man.'

Burns scowled horribly, but he knew when he was beaten. If he shot the preacher he would set all the better element in town against him. Already people were coming out of their shops and houses to see what was going on.

Glancing round at the watching gunmen and saloon loafers he saw that even those evil men were unlikely to support him if he went ahead and drew on the preacher. They had no time for preachers as preachers, but this one was a *man*!

'You win, Preacher!' he said reluctantly, straightening up from his gunfighter's crouch. 'You're a lucky man, King. But watch it in future. Next time you mayn't be so lucky!' He turned and swaggered off down the street towards the jail.

The mine-owner let out his pent-up breath in a long sigh of relief. He seized Hunter's hand and wrung it painfully, gabbling his thanks.

A moment later the two of them were surrounded by enthusiastic townspeople, all praising their new preacher's courage and wanting to pat him on the back.

Hunter accepted their praise with equanimity. 'It was nothing,' he said blandly. 'I just reminded your deputy what the Bible has to say about murder. The Word of God can soften even the hardest hearts. I hope you will all come to meeting on Sunday to hear the Word of God preached more fully.'

The townspeople slowly dispersed, excitedly talking over what they had just seen.

Hunter escorted George King back to the judge's house. 'You haven't any real proof that Ryker and his deputy are tied in with the Boot Hill Gang, have you, George?'

'Not a scrap. I just lost my temper and hit out at the nearest target. Losing four good men and all that gold sent me a little crazy, I guess.'

'If I were you I'd do as he says and keep out of town for a while,' Hunter advised him. 'Leave the search for the missing gold to me!'

4

All through dinner that evening Hunter was restless and ill at ease. The food was good, talk flowed freely and Stacy Barton as pretty a hostess as a man could wish for. But he could sense that God was calling him out into the darkened streets.

When the meal ended Hunter made his excuses and slipped away from the dining-room. Upstairs in his room he opened his bedroll and took out his gunbelt, cinching the worn black leather around his slim waist. Then with his ebony-handled Colt .44 riding in its holster on his right-hand side and his nine-inch Bowie knife resting comfortably against his left thigh he stole out of his room and tiptoed down the stairs.

But he couldn't move silently enough to prevent Stacy Barton's sharp ears from hearing him. As he crossed the hall towards the front door the sitting-room door opened and the pretty young woman slipped out.

'Where are you going, Mr Hunter?' she whispered.

'I don't know,' he replied softly. 'But God has told me that I'm needed out on the street tonight.'

'Then I won't try to stop you.' She glided forward and briefly pressed her lips against his cheek. 'But take care.'

'I shall,' said Hunter, turning his face away to hide the tide of red that suddenly deepened his tan. If he wasn't careful he would be falling in love with this girl.

His mouth twisted sourly. She was no girl, but a married woman, even if her husband had disappeared and was more than likely dead. And anyway, there was no room for a woman in his life.

Without saying another word he opened the door and slipped out.

By now it was fully dark, though the moon was due to rise above the surrounding hills any time soon. The Preacher kept to the shadows as he moved off down the street. He was sure that something was about to happen, but what?

The shopkeepers of Jackpot had all closed up their premises for the night, though the gleams of light finding their way round the edges of their blinds and curtains revealed that they and their families had not yet gone to bed. Further down the street the saloons and honky-tonks were ablaze with light.

Hunter moved along the boardwalk like a ghost. He slipped down the alleyway running between a saloon and the gunsmith's shop. At the back of the saloon was a big stack of empty barrels smelling of stale beer.

Suddenly a door opened at the back of the saloon and a man staggered out into the yard. The startled Hunter dived for cover behind a dray.

But the man wasn't looking for trouble. He groaned, clasping his stomach, then bent over and was comprehensively sick on to the dirty sand.

The Preacher grinned to himself in the darkness. 'Wine is a mocker,' he quoted silently, 'and strong drink is raging!' Leaving the drunken man to his misery he cat-footed off down the alley.

A little while later a new sound made him look round. A wagon was coming up the street, escorted by half a dozen riders. The sounds they made seemed oddly muffled.

Hunter shrank back into the shadows. As the little convoy rolled past he saw why it was making so little noise. All the horses' hooves had been wrapped with rags, as had the curb chains and other metal parts of the wagon.

The Preacher drew his gun and silently followed them. The convoy drew up outside an abandoned livery-stable on the outskirts of town. The man who had owned it had also operated a two-by-four claim up in the hills. He had been one of the first victims of the Boot Hill Gang. Now his barn was locked and deserted.

As the Preacher watched from the shelter of a tumbledown shanty across the way, one of the riders got down from his horse and fumbled in his vest pocket for a key. Then he opened the big double doors and stood aside as the wagon rolled in. The remaining riders followed, bowing their heads as they rode under the sagging lintel. Someone lighted a lamp inside the building. The doors swung to once more.

The Preacher ran silently across the alley and flattened himself against the wall of the building. Listening hard, Hunter heard a rough voice say, 'Right, you men. Get that gold unloaded as quick as you can.'

'And put it where, boss?' another voice asked.

'Stack it in the far stall. Cover it with straw. And be quick about it. We gotta be out of town before first light.'

'You ain't kiddin',' a third man said

with a chuckle. 'Makes me nervous, bein' this near to a sheriff.'

'You don't have to worry about Ryker,' a new voice said cynically. 'He don't go lookin' fer trouble. But if you take it to him, you better be real good with a gun.'

'How good?'

'Maybe Ben Thompson or Hardin could shade him a mite,' the cynical voice replied. 'But I'd hate to have to live on the difference.'

'Stop jawing and get on with the job!' the first voice said with a snap. 'I've never known such a mouthy lot of outlaws as you fellas.'

The other men raised a confused babble of protest. Why shouldn't they talk to each other? Hell, no one was listening to them!

The speaker's voice darkened menacingly. 'You sure of that? Better not take any chances. This racket's too good to spoil. Why, give him another six months and the big boss'll have the gold *and* own all the mines. Then we'll clean up.

But we ain't home and dry yet. So if I hear that anyone's been blabbing I'll give 'em to Whitey.'

The sudden silence that followed this remark told Hunter that this was no idle threat. But who or what was Whitey?

From the sounds that followed it was clear to the listening Hunter that the men had begun to unload the gold from the wagon and carry it into the stall. Their grunts of effort and muffled complaints about the weight of the bars came clearly to his ears.

Finally the job was done. 'What now, boss?' said an Irish voice tiredly.

'We take the wagon back where it came from; you stay here, on guard.'

'What the hell for, boss? A man'd have to be crazy to come into this old place, sure an' he would.'

'You'll stand guard, and that's that,' the leader snapped. 'A drunk could wander in here anytime, aiming to sleep it off in the straw. D'you *want* to risk losing the gold thataway?'

There was a tired chuckle in the Irish voice as he replied, 'Hell, no, boss. Not after what we done to get it!'

'I'll have some grub sent over to you later on. Pete here'll relieve you just before first light.'

There was a muffled groan of protest from the hidden Pete and a burst of mocking laughter from the other men.

'Quiet, you fools!' the boss man said sharply. 'Do you want to wake the whole town?' The laughter stopped as if cut off with a knife. Whoever this man was he had the authentic voice of command. 'We'll be back this time tomorrow night to fetch the gold away. Now, let's get out of here!'

That, Hunter told himself, was his cue to get out of there too. He ran across the alley and ducked down behind an old horse-trough.

Peering round the side of the trough he saw the doors open and the wagon rolled out into the street with two men on the seat. The other men followed the wagon on foot, leading their horses. The double doors swung to behind them. The riders mounted their horses and the whole convoy moved quietly away into the night.

The Preacher was amazed at the boldness of the gang. Bringing the gold into town was the action of men who thought they could do anything, anything at all, and get away with it. Well, they would soon learn different!

He made his way back to the judge's house without meeting anyone. Stacy Barton had gone to bed but the judge was still up, taking his ease in his study with a French novel and a glass of whiskey. When Hunter entered the room he hurriedly put the novel down on the floor beside his chair.

Hunter smiled to himself. Everyone expected a preacher to hold strong views about what was fit for a man to read and what wasn't.

Personally he couldn't give a damn. He was against censorship in all its forms. He'd never known a good man go bad as a result of reading a book or looking at a picture. It would make more sense to ban women and drink. Between them they'd sent many a good man to the Devil!

'I know where George King's missing gold has got to,' he began.

The judge nearly dropped his glass, he was so surprised.

'If he brings some of his men into town tomorrow evening he can take it back again. Maybe get the men who stole it and killed his employees, too.'

'But George has gone back to the Lynx,' the judge protested.

'I know. I told him to. Somehow he got on the wrong side of Deputy Sheriff Burns. Nearly got his fool head blown off. Burns was on the prod. Maybe he'll have cooled down by then. Maybe not. But I'm betting George'll take the risk, all the same.'

The judge chuckled. 'I guess you're right at that.'

When Hunter rode out of Jackpot he avoided the broad trail that led up to the Lynx mine. Instead he took the road that led to the county seat. After five or six miles he circled round to the north.

A couple of hours later he reached the crest of the hills and stopped for a moment or two to let his horse have a rest. While the animal cropped a handy bush he peered into the distance to try and get his bearings. A sparkle of light well over to his right indicated that the saloons, honky-tonks and bawdy-houses of Jackpot were still open for business although it was well after midnight. Ahead of him the land was dark. But that was the way he had to go.

He clicked his tongue softly. His horse recognized the signal and, snatching a last mouthful of leaves, moved off again.

Soon the smooth slope began to break up. The grass was replaced by patches of sand between outcrops of rock. Another mile and he was riding down a dry stream-bed with cliffs rising high on either side.

Not a place to be in if it rains! he thought ruefully, dismounting and leading his horse past a tangled mass of uprooted trees and other rubbish left behind by a flash-flood. The desert could kill you with too much water as well as too little!

Fortunately Hunter had recently examined a map of the country and had a good memory for detail. He also had a good sense of direction. He needed it. The land hereabouts was a maze of rocky valleys and blind canyons. They all ran down into the valley the miners called Jackpot Gulch. Hunter had chosen a route that would lead him out into the valley about a half a mile from the Lynx.

As the canyon he was riding down began to widen out and become somewhat less steep Hunter began to see dark holes in the rock on either side of the stream-bed with heaps of rubble and tailings beside them.

There were a few wooden shacks dotted about the hillside, but they all looked empty and abandoned. There were no lights; no smoke came from any of the tinpipe chimneys and many of their doors were swinging in the wind.

Nevertheless Hunter brought his horse to a halt and examined the little settlement carefully before going on. If any men were still living here they would be bound to be wary of strangers. And with the Boot Hill Gang on their backs who could blame them? Seeing a man on a horse, obviously no miner, they might well be tempted to shoot first and ask questions later.

Eventually he decided that the place was deserted, and urged his horse forward. The dry stream-bed twisted and turned between abandoned mines and derelict shacks. The moon was shining straight into the little valley and he could see almost as well as by day. The shadows were sharp and black.

In the clear night air he could hear the shallow waters of Rock Creek gurgling along somewhere down below him. He rounded a bluff and saw a two-room shack dug into the hillside on his left. It was larger than any of the other buildings he had seen so far, and unlike them its windows were shuttered and its door was securely fastened.

There was something about this shack that stirred Hunter's curiosity. It didn't have the same air of dereliction as the others he'd seen further up the canyon. Drawing his pistol he urged his horse towards it.

Leaning down from the saddle he grasped the latch and tried to lift it. It moved easily enough, but the door failed to open. Intrigued, Hunter took a match out of his top pocket and struck it on his saddle. In the brief seconds before the wind blew it out its flickering light showed him that the door was fastened with a large iron padlock.

Curiouser and curiouser, he thought. He guided his horse round the back of the building and discovered that it was hiding a mine. A pair of iron rails led into the tunnel, which was propped and beamed with timber. A large dump of mine tailings stood to one side of the rails, a smaller pile of ore to the other, handy for processing by a rusty ore crusher whose wooden handles reared stark arms against the sky. This was no hard-scrabble excavation like the ones operated by Gandy and Tin-Cup and their friends, this was a proper mine! Real money had been spent here.

Holstering his pistol, Hunter dismounted and picked up a handful of ore. Striking another match, he peered at the piece of rock, whistling softly at the veins of raw gold that threaded it. If all the ore was like this random sample the mine was a real bonanza! So why had it been abandoned? Had its owner been killed by the Boot Hill Gang?

Turning on his heel he walked from tie to tie between the iron rails to the mouth of the tunnel and stepped inside. Another match showed him that the shaft was properly timbered inside. He moved a few yards further in. The mine smelt dry and dusty. But there was another smell that made his nose wrinkle with distaste. He couldn't place it, but it was strangely familiar.

Some sixth sense suddenly warned him that he was not alone. He jumped back, and the point of a knife struck sparks from the rock wall of the mine where he had been standing only a moment before.

The unseen assassin cursed loudly and swung the knife again. Hunter recoiled, and heard the swish of air as the deadly blade swept past his throat.

He retreated another step, wondering what to do now. He could have pulled his gun and emptied the cylinder into the darkness ahead of him. Surely at least one of the bullets would have made a hit. But he felt oddly reluctant to do so. Did the unseen man need killing? He didn't know. The Preacher wasn't the man to kill if he didn't have to.

Hunter's eyes were beginning to adjust to the darkness now. He saw the gleam of red, feral eyes as his opponent came forward, knife raised. He stepped back. The ghostly knifeman swung, and missed once more.

With a whisper of metal on leather Hunter drew his own Bowie from its sheath at his belt. The nine-inch blade was made of the finest steel. It was so sharp that one full-bodied swing could cut a man's arm clean off.

Hunter raised the weapon and held it up in front of his face. Once again the knifeman slashed at Hunter. The two blades met with a loud ringing sound, followed by a sad tinkle as the broken blade of the man's knife fell to the rocky floor of the tunnel.

The shadowy knifeman gave a loud cry of anger and frustration, dropped the useless hilt and threw himself at Hunter. His hands closed round Hunter's throat with maniacal strength. Hot stinking breath beat into Hunter's face. Bony knees hammered at Hunter's thighs, aiming for the soft, defenceless groin.

He seemed to have forgotten that

Hunter was holding a Bowie and could have gutted him like a fish. But Hunter wanted to catch him, not kill him.

Hunter threw his Bowie behind him. Then he linked his two hands together and brought them up with all his strength. His fists smashed into his opponent's forearms with muscle-numbing force, driving them apart and breaking his unseen opponent's grip on his throat. Then he drove his iron-hard fists into his attacker's brisket three times in quick succession.

The man gasped with pain and staggered backwards, then tripped over the iron rails and fell with a crash to the floor.

Hunter came forward cautiously, one hand feeling ahead of him in the darkness, one fist drawn back, cocked and ready. Fighting in the pitch darkness of the mineshaft was a dangerous game.

His would-be assassin gave a snarl of frustration and baffled hatred, then turned and scrambled away into the darkness. The sounds that followed made it clear that he was scuttling deeper into the hill.

Hunter wasn't about to to follow him down there! He bent down and fumbled around for his hat, which had fallen off in the struggle. It took him much longer to find his Bowie.

Five minutes later he rode out of the mouth of Rock Creek into Jackpot Gulch. Half a mile to his right he could see the buildings and other structures surrounding the shaft of the mine owned by George King and called by him the Lynx.

The mine itself was dark, but although it was nigh on midnight, lights were still showing in a number of smaller buildings on the site. The whole area was ringed by a split-log fence with a wide gate in it, big enough for a wagon to go through. Hunter rode up to the gate and waited.

After a few seconds a voice spoke out of the darkness. 'What d'you want, stranger?'

'To see Mr King. On business.'

'Do you now? And would *he* want to see you?'

Hunter smiled to himself in the darkness. 'I think so. Now are you going to let me in, or are you going to get him to come out here?'

There was a click as the gate guard unmasked a bull's-eye lantern and turned a powerful beam on Hunter, who quickly turned his head to hide his face. But the man behind the light was more interested in examining the stranger's hands than in identifying him. Then he played the yellow beam over Hunter's body, lingering on his belt gun and the rifle under his knee.

'Shuck your guns, mister, then come ahead if you've got a mind to,' the voice commanded sternly.

Hunter unbuckled his gunbelt and let it fall, then slid his Winchester .44-40 from its boot and lowered it to the ground.

'Walk on!' the hidden guard instructed him. At the same moment a bell rang faintly inside the house. Hunter presumed that the guard had activated it in some way. Well, at least they would be expecting him. He nudged his horse's flanks with his spurs and trotted up to the house.

The door opened and two men with shotguns burst out and broke left and right, swinging the muzzles of their guns to focus on Hunter. He hoped they were good men, steady on the trigger. If all four barrels let go at once they would have to scrape him off the sand with a shovel!

Then the tall, thin figure of George King came out on to the stoop. He peered into the darkness.

'That you, Mr . . . ?'

'That's right!' Hunter said quickly. 'No names, though. You know why!'

The mine-owner told his two guards to put up their guns, then stepped down off the stoop and walked up to Hunter. 'We better keep our voices down,' he said in a low voice.

'So we should,' Hunter agreed.

'What are you doin' here?' The mine-owner sounded puzzled. Then his voice changed. 'Have you found my missing gold?'

Hunter chuckled richly. 'I sure have. It's just waiting for you to take it away!' He cut short the babble of questions that rose to George King's lips by asking, 'But you'll need some men you can trust. Really trust!'

The mine-owner knew what he was getting at. Someone at the mine must have tipped off the Boot Hill Gang that a gold shipment was being made that day.

'I've thought long and hard about that,' he said soberly. 'It's gotta to be one of my clerks. The workmen didn't know we was shipping gold into town until we started loading the bars on to the wagon. I've got the site locked up tight. They had no chance to get the news out. But the clerks knew about it more'n a week ago. Any one of 'em could have spilled the beans!'

'Keep this from them then,' Hunter

replied quietly. 'The Boot Hill Gang feel so safe they hid your gold in town. There's only one man guarding it. The rest of the robbers are coming back to collect it after dark.'

He told King what he had seen and heard.

The mine-owner began to splutter his thanks. Hunter cut him off. 'Listen, George,' he said. 'Eight or ten of the gang came into town with the gold. I'd like to catch them red-handed with the loot. That'd give the judge the chance to try them according to law and then hang them legally. The townspeople have lost faith in the law. They think the Boot Hill Gang can get away with anything. Let's show them different, eh!'

George King rubbed his jaw thoughtfully. 'The miners are Polacks, mostly. Good fighters, but only with their fists and boots, not guns. The Gang already shot my best guards. But I could raise maybe six men who can use a gun.' He paused, then went on with a funny little gulp, 'Including me, that is!'

'Good man!' Hunter said approvingly. 'Send them into town in pairs. Tell them to keep out of trouble. We'll meet up in the shanty across the way from the old livery-stable at dusk. OK?'

The mine-owner swallowed nervously. 'We'll be there,' he said valiantly.

Hunter swung his horse's head round to face the gate. 'Your man will give me back my guns, I trust,' he said with a chuckle.

'Give the man his guns and let him out!' King called into the darkness.

'Right you are Mr King,' came the reply.

Hunter leaned out of the saddle to whisper into the mine-owner's ear. 'You won't see me tomorrow, but you'll hear me. Tell your men to do what I say.'

'I will.'

'And don't bother to bring a wagon for the gold,' Hunter added with a low chuckle. 'The Boot Hill Gang will be doing that for you!'

He touched his spurs to his horse's

flanks and trotted over to the gate, which the guard had already swung open. The man was standing in the gap, holding Hunter's rifle and gunbelt. Hunter took them from him, slid the rifle into its boot, buckled his gunbelt round his waist, then rode off into the darkness.

5

The next day was Sunday. After breakfast, the Preacher went down to the church. He put his Bible on the lectern and opened it at his text for the day, then gazed out over the rows of empty benches.

Would he get a good congregation? He had done his best to encourage the townsmen and their families to attend, also the miners and their families. But the Devil had a strong grip on Jackpot. He had already driven one preacher out of town, using the saloon roughs as his instruments. Maybe he would try it again!

He walked back down the aisle to the porch and hauled on the bellrope. High over his head the big bronze bell stirred from its slumbers.

Clang! Clang! the summons rang out over the little town. *Clang! Clang!*

That ought to wake them up! The Preacher hooked up the bellrope and went back to the lectern to wait.

The first person to arrive was the woman whose husband he'd saved from the two gunmen on his arrival in town, and her children. She told them to sit down at the back, then hurried down the aisle towards him. 'Any news of my Reuben, Preacher?' she whispered urgently.

'None, thank the Lord,' Hunter replied softly.

The woman's face showed her dismay. Hunter smiled reassuringly. 'Take it from me, Mrs Wilson. No news is good news. Trust in the Lord and all will be well. Now take a seat and remember' — he shut one eye — 'you don't know me.'

The woman nodded. 'I get it. I'll tell the kids.' She went back to her seat and whispered urgently to her children.

A group of townspeople came in next, including jovial Fred Yerko, the gunsmith, and his wife and ten children, Euan McGregor, the dour Scots livery-stable operator and his sallow, barren wife, and Humbert Ross, the proprietor of the town's best hotel, with his wife and three strapping daughters. Unnoticed by either set of parents, one of the gunsmith's sons began to flirt with Ross's eldest daughter.

More women from the poorer end of town came in with their children and joined Mrs Wilson at the back of the church. To Hunter's faint surprise some of them had brought their menfolk with them. The miners' heavy boots clattered on the wooden boards as they made their way to their places.

Hunter was sourly amused by the way the church divided. The towns-people, shopkeepers and the like, all sat towards the front. The men were wearing smart suits and white shirts with stiff collars. Their womenfolks had dressed in their Sunday-go-to-meeting best.

They examined each other's dresses

and hats critically, but said nothing, saving up their barbed comments for use at sewing bees and other events where gossip was welcomed. They turned up their noses at the shabby miners and their dowdy women and scruffy children sitting at the back of the church.

Slowly the church filled up. Looking out over the sea of faces Hunter wondered how many of these people came to church regularly. Not many, he thought. Most of them would have come out of curiosity. Small-town life was pretty unexciting at the best of times. The arrival of a new preacher was an major event!

Jolly Jack Reeve came in, nodded to the Preacher and sat down on the front bench. It creaked under his weight.

Hunter took his watch from his waistcoat pocket and consulted it. Only one minute to ten o'clock. Where were Judge Chaffee and Stacy Barton? Weren't they coming to hear him preach?

Just as the minute hand reached the hour, Stacy came in, followed by the judge. Stacy was dressed with an understated elegance that put to shame the elaborate dresses and hats the shopkeepers' wives were wearing. She looked every inch a lady as she traipsed down the aisle and took her seat in front of the lectern.

The judge sat beside her. His eyes met Hunter's. Their message was clear. He would back the Preacher all the way!

Hunter had given a lot of thought to the shape of the service. Out here in the West preachers of any stripe were few and far between, and Catholics and Baptists, Episcopalians and Methodists, members of a hundred sects and honest seekers after faith all attended the same Sunday Meeting.

When the land filled up and the town grew bigger, each denomination would want to build its own church and employ its own preacher, but right now he had to cater for everyone.

One thing everybody loved was a good sing-song. It bound them together. So after introducing himself and welcoming them to the church he announced the first hymn.

The town's schoolmistress, an acid-tongued and prune-faced maiden lady, took her seat at the battered harmonium in the corner. Her feet pumped at the pedals. The machine groaned protestingly as the pressure built up. Then she brought her hands down hard on the keys and off they went: 'Rock of Ages, cleft for me . . . '

When the hymn came to an end the Preacher announced his text. It came from Psalm 37, and began: 'For yet a little while and the wicked shall not be!'

There was hiss of indrawn breath from his congregation. They could guess what was coming next. Sure enough he began to preach against the Boot Hill Gang. Drawing on a wide range of Biblical quotations to support his case that God often intervened to save his people from their oppressors he promised a swift end to the troubles that were afflicting Jackpot and its nearby mining district.

As soon as the Preacher was fairly into his stride a couple of flashily dressed men sitting at the back got up and sidled out of the door.

Gone to report to their master, he supposed. That meant trouble. And soon.

But nothing had happened by the time the service came to an end. While his congragation were gathering their traps and getting to their feet Hunter strode down the aisle and took up his position in the porch to wish them goodbye.

The miners and their families, having been sitting at the back of the church, were first to leave.

'Damn good sermon, Preacher,' said one man roughly.

'Real fightin' talk!' confirmed another. 'You a fighter, Mr Walker? Or was it all hot air?'

Hunter smiled back at the man, but

his eyes were hard. 'I can fight if I have to.'

'Just as well, I'd say.' Fred Yerko pushed to the front. 'Has anyone told you what happened to Preacher Hernshaw!'

'They did! *And* that none of you men tried to help him!'

'Of course we didn't!' the gunsmith said aggressively. 'We ain't gunmen. That's Ryker's job! It's what we pay him for, ain't it?'

There was a murmur of agreement on all sides.

'Then if he isn't doing it, why not get rid of him?' Hunter asked ingenuously.

A silence followed this remark. It was obviously a very unwelcome suggestion. Fred Yerko had no answer to it. Head averted, he pushed past Hunter and plunged out of the building. His wife and children hurried after him.

That broke the log-jam, and one by one the members of the congregation came up to Hunter and mumbled their goodbyes, then left the church. Five minutes later the only people still in the building were the judge, Stacy Barton, Jolly Jack Reeve and Hunter himself.

'Well, you sure told 'em,' grinned Jolly Jack.

Hunter shrugged dismissively. 'I don't suppose it'll do any good. The ones who aren't scared stiff of the Boot Hill Gang are frightened of crossing Ryker.'

'You can't blame them too much,' said the judge deprecatingly. 'They did try to clean up the town by appointing Ryker sheriff. OK, that didn't work too well. Next they set up the vigilantes. That got three of the best and bravest of them killed. So now they just don't want to know.' His lips twitched in a wry smile. 'It's up to us now.'

The church door banged open and six burly saloon loafers pushed their way into the building. Each man carried a brand new pickaxe handle. Three of them were dressed in miners' clothes, threadbare and caked with mud. Two wore faded jeans and linsey-woolsey shirts. Long ago, before the drink got to them, they had been cowhands.

They were led by a great bull of a man six foot six in his socks with shoulders to match. He was dressed in town duds that were only slightly the worse for wear. He hefted his club and took a pace forward.

'Get out, Judge,' he said roughly, 'and take the lady with you. You too, Jolly Jack. We got no quarrel with you!'

'It's with me, then,' the Preacher said blandly.

'Right ye are, Preacher,' the man chuckled nastily. 'Yer bin shootin' yer mouf off, just like Preacher Hernshaw used ter do. We showed him the error of his ways. Now it's your turn!'

He slapped his pickaxe handle into his meaty palm suggestively. One of his companions ogled Stacy's shapely figure and whistled lasciviously. Another one made an obscene motion with his stave.

The judge didn't like to leave Hunter

to the tender mercies of these thugs, not even for a minute, but Stacy's safety came first. 'Come with me, Stacy,' he said reluctantly.

'I'm not leaving!' she said resolutely.

'Yes, you are,' snapped the judge, and grasped her firmly by the arm. He turned his head and met Hunter's eye. 'I'll be back,' he whispered.

Stacy Barton was stronger than she looked. Sensing that the judge's attention was distracted she jerked her arm free from his grip, neatly dodged his grasping arms and flattened herself against the back wall of the church. 'I'm not leaving this good man to face his enemies alone,' she said defiantly. 'Now are you going to stay and help him?'

The six thugs had been watching all this with amusement. Now their leader spoke again. 'Likes to watch, does she? Well, that's OK by me. Maybe we can think of something she'll like even better, when this is all over.'

He gestured lewdly with his club. His men sniggered loudly. 'You two gents goin' or stayin'?'

The judge glanced at Jolly Jack. 'As the man says, are you going or staying?'

''And who will stand on either hand and keep the bridge with me?'' quoted Jolly Jack, and shook a life-preserver from his sleeve. Its lead-weighted head was set on a flexible whalebone shaft and the whole thing was covered with a woven leather sheath. He slipped the thong over his wrist and took a firm grip of the handle. 'I guess I'll stick. You?'

The judge was lame in one leg and walked with the aid of an ebony walking-stick. Now he took the shaft in both hands, twisted sharply, then pulled. The stick came apart, leaving him holding two and a half feet of shining steel in his right hand and the hollow shaft of the stick in his left.

Eyebrows raised, Hunter glanced from Jolly Jack's life-preserver to the judge's sword-stick.

'You're a fine pair of law-abiding citizens!' he chuckled, reaching over to take the thin ebony shaft from the judge's left hand. It was almost three feet long and heavy, with a brass ferrule on one end. 'This'll do me,' he said appreciatively.

The six thugs had been taken aback by this unexpected turn of events. They had been paid to give a defenceless man a beating. Now they were facing three men, all of them armed. But they had been paid to do a job, and weren't about to back out just because it had suddenly become a mite harder than they had expected.

'Let's get 'em, boys,' spat the leader of the group of thugs and advanced ponderously down the aisle, flanked on either side by one of his companions. The other three men hung back to give them room to swing their clubs. The aisle was too narrow for all six of them to walk abreast.

The leader swung his club at Hunter with all his force. If it had reached its target it would have caved in Hunter's skull like an egg. But Hunter swayed aside. The weapon hissed past his shoulder and smashed into the front bench, splintering the wood badly.

Before the tough could recover his balance Hunter drove the ferrule end of his stick into his belly with all his strength. The bully-boy doubled up with a groan of anguish.

Hunter spun the stick and brought it down with measured force on the nape of his opponent's neck. The little wooden church shuddered as the massive body dropped senseless to the floor.

The thug who faced Jolly Jack had no doubts about his ability to smash the grinning fat man into a leaking pile of lard. A life-preserver was a fine weapon at close quarters, but it was far outranged by his three-foot club. And his arms were a lot longer than Jolly Jack's.

He swung his pickaxe handle in short arcs in front of his body, driving Jolly Jack back and back before it. There was no way that the fat man could strike at him with his shorter weapon without being clobbered.

Or so he thought. He had forgotten, if he ever knew, that short fat men are often amazingly swift and light on their feet. Watch them dancing at any hoe-down and you'll see that it's true.

The bully-boy swung his club hard to the left. Jolly Jack swayed away from the stroke, then pranced forward and tapped his opponent on the temple with his life-preserver. The blow seemed light, almost casual, but the man dropped like a puppet whose strings had been cut.

The third thug approached the judge warily. He didn't like the look of the old man's toadsticker. 'Don't be a fool, Judge,' he said roughly. 'You don't have to get hurt. Just put that spike down and get outa here.'

The judge had been a fine swordsman in his youth. He had killed three men in duels. Now he welcomed the chance to prove that he wasn't too old to increase the total to four. He snapped into the on-guard position. 'If you want it, come and take it,' he drawled menacingly, flexing his wrist and sending the point of his sword flickering towards the man's throat.

The bully-boy shuddered away from the flashing steel, then swung his club up with all his strength, hoping to catch the judge's sword-arm and either break it or knock the sword from his hand.

It was a bad mistake. Ignoring his creaking joints and his bad back the judge bent at the knees and the club whistled safely over his head. Then he lunged. The sword slid between the man's ribs and pierced his right lung.

The unshaven saloon loafer looked down at the thin blade transfixing his chest with horrified eyes. He coughed wetly and blood appeared on his lips. He staggered and his club fell from his nerveless fingers.

The judge pulled his sword from the wound. A gush of blood promptly stained the man's shirt. More blood gushed out of his mouth and trickled down his chin. He swayed backwards and forwards and then fell on his face with a crash.

The three surviving bully-boys exchanged worried glances. They had been recruited from the saloons and honky-tonks with the promise of a gold piece in exchange for a little fighting. But now their leader was down, maybe dead. Who would pay them now?

Hunter gestured with his stick. 'We're ready when you are, gentlemen,' he said blandly.

The three men scowled. Then one spoke up. He had a heavy Scandinavian accent. 'We're goin'. We din't bargain fer no killin'. A beatin', but no killin'.' There was unwilling respect in his voice as he added, 'You three fellers sure can fight, by jiminy!'

'Next time you go out on a job like this, you'd better be sure your sheep aren't wolves in disguise,' Hunter said coldly. 'Even better, change your ways altogether.'

'You beat us fair and square, mister,'

one of the other men said sourly, 'don't preach at us too.'

Hunter chuckled and spread his hands wide. 'Why not? Isn't this the place for it?'

'Damn you, Preacher!' the third man said bitterly. He clumped heavily towards the door. The other two men followed his lead.

'Wait!' barked Hunter. 'Who sent you?'

The first two men ignored him, plunging through the door and away. The Scandinavian lingered for a moment in the doorway. 'I dunno,' he said resentfully. 'But I hopes they gets you next time.' He raised his arm and threw his club at Hunter, then whipped through the door and was gone.

'Well, that was fun, while it lasted,' said Jolly Jack with a grin, tucking his life-preserver back up his sleeve.

The judge agreed. 'Maybe I'm not so old as I thought,' he said smugly, wiping his blade on his victim's linsey-woolsey shirt. Hunter handed him his ebony cane and he slid the thin sword blade into it. A quick twist of the wrist and the stick was again whole and innocent-looking.

Stacy Barton came from her place by the altar and, almost crying with relief that the fight was over and none of them had been hurt, hugged each man in turn, starting with the judge and ending with Hunter.

Was there an added pressure in her embrace? the Preacher wondered, then hurriedly told himself that he was imagining it.

Stacy's foot accidentally touched one of the bodies and she gave a little scream. 'Are they all dead?' she gasped.

Jolly Jack grasped the tangled hair of the man he had fought and lifted up his head. The saloon loafer had a bloody dent in the side of his head you could put half an apple in. 'Dead as mutton!' he said with satisfaction.

The judge didn't even need to look at his victim. He knew where his blade had gone. 'Mine too,' he confirmed.

Hunter had struck, so he hoped, with just enough force to knock his opponent out, but not kill him. He wanted to ask him who had hired the six of them to give him a beating.

He bent down and grasped the thug by the shoulder and turned him over. The man was still breathing, but he was out for the count and his face had turned a nasty shade of puce.

'Doesn't look too healthy, does he?' said Jolly Jack with a grin. 'I guess you don't know your own strength, Preacher.'

'We better take him over to Doc Sandilands' right away,' said the judge. 'It's not too far.'

'Then I'll carry him,' said the Preacher. 'Help me get him on my back, will you?'

The unconscious thug was a dead weight but between them they managed it. Bearing his heavy burden Hunter staggered down the aisle. The judge followed, then Stacy, and Jolly Jack brought up the rear.

Outside in the street the sunlight was blinding after the relative gloom of the church. The man on Hunter's back seemed to weigh a ton. The Preacher staggered along, bent almost double under the weight, while the sweat rolled down his forehead and ran into his eyes.

'It's not much further,' said Jolly Jack encouragingly.

'Thank God for that,' muttered Hunter. 'I don't think I *could* carry him much further.'

He didn't have to.

Boom!

A shot rang out, loud in the Sunday quiet, and a bullet smashed into the man on the Preacher's back. Hunter was thrown off-balance by the impact. He pitched forward and fell to the sand with the heavy body on top of him.

The gunman did not fire again.

Hunter's three friends rolled the bloody corpse aside, half expecting to see the Preacher lying dead on the sand beneath it. But although bruised and covered with dirt, their friend was unhurt. Sighing with relief, they helped him to his feet.

By now a crowd had gathered. 'You all right, Preacher?' a member of his recent congregation said with obvious concern.

'Fine, thank you,' Hunter replied politely, brushing the sand from his clothes with his hat. Then he inspected the body. The deadly bullet had struck the unconscious man between the shoulderblades and silenced him forever.

'Who's the deader?' Humbert Ross inquired curiously.

'His name's Ryan. Worked over at the Bon Ton,' a flashily dressed gambler replied with a shrug. 'Swamping, chucking out, you name it he'd do it, as long as there was drinking money in it!'

Burt Ryker bullied his way through the crowd. 'What's bin goin' on?' he said, squaring up to Hunter aggressively. 'You kill this man, Preacher?'

'How could I?' The preacher spread

his coat-tails, showing everyone that he wasn't wearing a gun. He grinned tiredly at the burly sheriff. 'Anyway, I was carrying him on my back at the time.'

'Why the hell were you doin' that?' the sheriff said suspiciously.

'He was taking this man to Doc Sandilands',' said the judge. 'The man was unconscious and needed medical attention. But someone shot him first!'

'What kind of sheriff are you, anyway, Mr Ryker?' Stacy said crossly. 'A man has been shot down in the street like a dog and all you do is ask stupid questions! Why aren't you looking for the killer?'

There was a murmur of approval from the townsfolk. They admired the judge's feisty young niece's courage in coming all the way from St Louis in an attempt to find her missing husband. The fact that she was beautiful didn't hurt either.

Sheriff Ryker scowled and shuffled his feet. 'OK,' he said sourly. 'Where'd the bullet come from? Anyone see the gunman? Anyone see anything?'

The ensuing silence was broken by the Preacher. 'I was on my way from the church, Sheriff. So as the bullet hit the poor fellow in the back I imagine it must have come from that direction.'

Everyone turned to look that way. The church was the only substantial building at that end of town. The rest were shacks and lean-tos. The shot could have come from any one of them.

The burly sheriff sighed heavily. 'He'll be long gone by now, I guess. But I'll have a look, just the same.' Then a thought seemed to strike him. 'What was wrong with Ryan anyway, Preacher?'

'Concussion.'

The sheriff's craggy face showed his astonishment. 'And how did *that* happen?'

Hunter's face gave nothing away. 'Some men tried to treat me the way they treated Parson Hernshaw. He was one of them. Mr Reeve and the judge

134

helped me drive them off.'

'And this man was the only one hurt?'

Hunter looked mildly embarrassed. 'Not exactly. The judge killed one of them and Mr Reeve another. The other three fled.'

The sheriff pushed back his battered Stetson and scratched his head distractedly. 'And you knocked the other man out, did you, Preacher?'

'Why yes,' Hunter replied innocently. 'I wouldn't want to kill a man inside my church.'

Ryker shot him a suspicious glance from under his heavy brows. Was the preacher secretly laughing at him?

'What should I do about the bodies, Sheriff?' Hunter said, looking concerned. 'They can't stay in my church.'

The sheriff looked round. As usual the black-clad undertaker was hovering on the fringes of the crowd. He crooked his finger. 'Hey, Widdowson! Take this body over to your place, then fetch the others from the church.'

The undertaker put two fingers in his mouth and whistled shrilly. His assistant came running up pushing a two-wheeled bier. The crowd hastily cleared a path through to the body.

Between them the two sober-suited ghouls loaded the body on to the bier and rolled it away.

'Bury them tomorrow, if you like.' Ryker's lip curled. 'That's another fifteen dollars you've earned, Preacher. Doin' well out of Jackpot, ain't you?'

Without giving Hunter a chance to reply he turned on his heel and stumped off down the street.

Jolly Jack shook the Preacher by the hand. 'I enjoyed your sermon, preacher,' he said with an irrepressible grin. 'And what came after. I used to think Sunday Meeting was dull. Now I know different!'

Still grinning, he made his farewells to Stacy and the judge and trotted off down the street to his general store.

Stacy Barton linked her arm in Hunter's and they and the judge walked slowly back to the big white house for lunch. Behind them the crowd slowly broke up.

Five minutes later the street was empty save for a scrawny dog licking hungrily at the pool of spilt blood.

6

As darkness fell on the town of Jackpot, Jolly Jack Reeve strode down the street towards the judge's house. He knocked on the front door and was admitted by the judge's efficient manservant.

Hunter and the judge were waiting for him inside the house. Both men were dressed for war. The judge had changed into the clothes he normally used for hunting and was toting one of the latest model Winchester repeaters. The Preacher was wearing range clothes, moccasins instead of boots, a black shirt instead of a white one and had smeared his face and hands with soot.

Jolly Jack raised his eyebrows. Rigged out like that the Preacher would be able to slip though the night like a ghost. As if he had picked up the thought the Preacher drew his Bowie and ran his thumb down the edge of the blade.

The storekeeper shuddered. He sure wouldn't want to be a member of the Boot Hill Gang tonight! The Angel of Death had come to Jackpot!

The door opened and Stacy Barton came in. She smiled warmly at the judge, greeted Jack Reeve as the old friend he was, and said with a lift of her delicate chin: 'And why have you covered your face with soot, Mr Hunter?'

The judge spoke for him. 'So that it won't show in the dark, my dear.'

'Then I can't wish *you* luck the way I was going to, now, can I?' she said gaily to the Preacher. She leaned forward and pecked at the judge's cheek, then Jolly Jack's. 'Don't fail to claim it when you get back!'

The Preacher hesitated. What was he getting himself into? Then he shrugged slightly. 'All right, Mrs Barton, I will.'

Stacy flushed, registering the reproof. He was right. She was a married woman. She ought not to be flirting with anyone, let alone a preacher. But there was something about this man that made her feel all girlish and frisky.

Hunter gave her no time to recover. He turned away from her and spoke to the two men. 'I'll go first. There may be a watcher. If so, I'll deal with him. Wait by the door until I give you the OK.'

They nodded soberly. Hunter's words were a sentence of death for anyone lurking out there in the darkness. The Preacher turned on his heel and went out of the room. They followed, leaving Stacy to wait and worry until they returned.

Hunter walked down the darkened passage leading to the back door of the judge's house and slipped out into the yard. The moon hadn't yet risen above the hills looming over the town and the darkness was absolute.

The night was alive with sound. The saloons were clearly doing good business. The tinny jangle of half a dozen pianos rose above the dull roar of drunken voices. Donkeys brayed, horses neighed, pots and pans clattered, children cried and women yelled at their erring husbands. The normal sounds of town life in the West.

Hunter flattened himself against the wall of the building and let his eyes adjust to the darkness and his ears adjust to the level of background noise. Soon he was able to distinguish the darker shape of the buildings across the way against the sky.

Was anyone watching the judge's house? If Hunter had been bossing the Boot Hill Gang he would have had someone keep an eye on the place for sure.

He stood quite still for what seemed like an age, breathing gently through his mouth, listening to the sounds of the night.

Finally he decided that the coast was clear. He was about to move off when he heard the faintest whisper of sound. It came from close at hand.

He froze, hardly daring to breathe.

There it came again. The sound

puzzled him at first, then the explanation came to him in a blinding flash. It was the sound produced by a man's trouserlegs rubbing together as he shifted his weight from foot to foot.

Peering into the darkness, Hunter soon found the watcher. The man was standing in the doorway of the abandoned shack across the way. Hunter had carefully examined the area in daylight and knew that the shack was about forty feet away.

His jaw tightened. There was no way he could get away from his present position without being seen. The man would have to be killed.

But how? It had to be done silently. The man had been positioned there to give the alarm if anyone left the judge's house by the back way. The slightest noise might bring more men coming at a run.

That meant using the knife. Hunter chewed his lip doubtfully. Forty feet was a long way to throw a knife accurately.

But he had to take the chance. Slowly and with infinite care the Preacher drew his Bowie from its sheath. He would only get one chance at this. It would have to be perfect.

He silently prayed for help and for forgiveness. Then his arm whipped down with the speed of a striking snake. The heavy blade flew across the yard and thudded home in the man's chest.

The gunman gasped, clutched feebly at the black bone handle protruding from his shirtfront, and sank slowly to the ground.

Hunter tapped softly on the door behind him. It opened and the judge stuck his head out. 'Is it safe?' the white-haired old man whispered softly.

'It is now.'

Hunter cat-footed across the forty feet of open ground and knelt beside his victim. The man was already dead. The Preacher silently said a prayer for the soul of the departed gang member, then pulled his knife from the man's chest, wiped the bloody blade on his victim's horse-hide vest and slipped it back into its sheath.

Hunter and Jolly Jack dragged the body into the shack and closed the door on it. With God's help it wouldn't be found for a while.

That done, the three men set off for the meeting-place. They kept to the back streets, ducking into the shadows whenever they saw someone approaching and staying quite still until the townsman, miner or cowboy had gone by.

George King was waiting inside the tumbledown shanty. He looked nervous, but determined. He had five well-armed men with him. As the judge pushed open the door they raised their guns.

George was holding a bull's-eye lantern. He uncovered it and trained the beam of light on the judge.

'Dowse that light!' snapped Hunter from the darkness outside the door. The mine-owner hastened to obey.

Jolly Jack followed the judge into the

shanty. 'Evening, George,' he said gaily. 'Ready for action?'

'We're here, ain't we?' George said resentfully. He wasn't used to people speaking to him as sharply as Hunter had done.

The Preacher entered the building and shut the door behind him. Now the darkness was absolute. They could hear each other breathing and the faint scrape of boots on the dirt floor, but that was all.

'I'll go and silence the watchman in the barn,' said Hunter, 'then call you over. When the Boot Hill Gang turns up to collect the gold you'll have the drop on them.'

'What about you? Where'll you be, mister?' asked one of King's men suspiciously.

'Out here, making sure none of them gets away! Now wait here until I call!'

Quiet as a snake he slipped out of the shanty, picked his way across the rutted alleyway and pressed himself against the warped and sundried boards of the abandoned livery stable.

Hunter drifted on silent feet all round the building, looking for the back door. Reaching it, he tried the handle, but the door was locked.

There was only one way to get in. He would have to trick the guard into opening the main door.

Returning to the front of the building he knocked softly on the timbers. 'Pete! Open up, for Christ's sake!' he whispered.

Straw rustled within the building as the man inside got up and came towards the door. Light shone brightly through the gaps in the planks. Pete was carrying a lantern in his hand.

Hunter drew his Colt .44 but left it uncocked, worried that Pete would hear the metallic click and refuse to open up.

'Who's there?' demanded Pete.

'Nick!' Hunter replied harshly. The name belonged to one of the other men in the gang. Hunter had heard it mentioned while they were hiding the gold. He was doing his best to imitate the gunman's throaty voice.

It seemed to convince Pete, anyway, for he replied: 'What are you doin' here, Nick?'

'Thought you might like a shot of rye,' Hunter replied with a throaty chuckle. 'It's mighty dry work, guardin' a dusty stable, I'm thinkin'.'

'You ain't just a woofin',' Pete replied plaintively. 'This danged hole is as full of dust as a hound has fleas. I been sneezin' fit to beat the band.'

Hunter heard the clatter of bolts being withdrawn. Then the door opened a couple of feet and Pete's unshaven face appeared in the gap.

'Hey! You ain't Nick . . . ' he gasped.

Before he could shut the door Hunter brought his gun from behind his back and thrust it under Pete's chin, cocking the hammer with his thumb as he did so. The metallic click was loud in the night. 'Silence, if you value your life!' he said sharply.

Pete nodded his head frantically.

'Back up!'

Step by step Pete retreated into the stable. Hunter followed him closely, never allowing the muzzle of his gun to move an inch from the guard's throat, not even when he reached behind him with his disengaged hand and pushed the big door shut.

Hunter took Pete's gun from its holster and tossed it on to a pile of stale straw in a corner. Then he lowered his pistol, though he still kept it trained on the terrified man.

Hunter was quite sure that his face, smeared as it was with soot, was unrecognizable. Otherwise he would have had to kill the man. As it was . . . 'Turn round,' he ordered.

Pete did as he was told.

The Preacher uncocked his Colt. Swiftly reversing his grip on the weapon, he crashed the butt down on the defenceless man's skull. Pete dropped without a groan.

Replacing his pistol in its holster, the Preacher picked up the lantern and walked over to the big double doors.

Opening the left-hand door he swung the lantern from side to side three times, then put it down on the floor and stepped back into the sheltering darkness.

One by one the men waiting in the shanty across the way ran over to the livery stable. Hunter recognized the mine-owner's two bodyguards. They wore belt guns and carried shotguns. The other three were dressed in miners' duds. They had pistols shoved through their belts and carried ex-Army Springfields. All five looked hard as nails.

The judge pointed the barrel of his Winchester at the man on the floor. 'Is he dead?'

Hunter's voice came coldly from the darkness. 'No. He'll live to be hanged. Someone better tie him up, though.'

One of George King's silent bodyguards found an old piece of harness hanging on a nail and tied the man up, then rolled him into an empty stall out of the way.

'Where's my gold?' George King asked eagerly.

'In the corner, under a heap of stale straw.'

The mine-owner rushed over to the heap and began feverishly to pull great bunches of the soursmelling stuff away with his hands. In seconds he had exposed a pile of iron-bound strongboxes. He counted them greedily.

'It's all here!' he gloated. 'It's all here!'

'Quiet, you fool!' said the judge. 'Do you want the gang to hear you? They'll be arriving any time now!'

George King flushed bright red. 'Sorry,' he mumbled. 'I got carried away there for a moment.'

' "Therefore did my heart rejoice, and my tongue was glad',' the Preacher remarked with a chuckle.

The men from the mine looked at his shadowy figure curiously. Who *was* this man? Their employer took his orders. So did the judge and Jolly Jack. He had silenced the guard as easy as pie. Now he was spouting phrases from the Book.

'Choose your places and get ready for

action,' Hunter told them. 'The judge will tell you what to do.' He had given the judge detailed instructions earlier that day. 'And God be with you.'

He put the lantern down on the floor inside the building and shut the door on them.

'He's a strange one,' one of the miners grunted to his partner.

The other snorted. 'Maybe so. But I'm mighty glad he's on our side.'

'Shut up, Rory,' hissed their employer. 'You too, Jacob.'

'Yes, boss.'

The straw rustled as the five men found what shelter they could behind the rotting timbers of the abandoned stable and hunkered down to wait for the Boot Hill Gang to show up.

On the far side of the street the Preacher leaned against the wall of the shanty and whispered the words of the seventy-first psalm to himself under his breath They seemed mighty appropriate just then.

Half an hour later, a rider came into

view at the end of the street. Two more followed him, then a wagon with two men on the box, then two more riders. The wagon made hardly any sound as it rolled slowly up the street towards the livery stable, and Hunter assumed that as on the previous occasion both the horses' hooves and the ironwork of the wagon had been muffled with rags.

Clearly none of the men was expecting any trouble. Their guns were in their holsters and they were chatting to each other in low, cheerful voices as they rode along.

Hunter stepped back through the open door into the darkness of the shanty as the convoy pulled up outside the livery-stable.

One of the riders called softly, 'Pete! Open up!'

The big double doors swung slowly back. The yellow light of the lantern spilled out into the street. The first three riders trotted into the budding, ducking their heads to clear the lintel. The driver flicked his reins and the wagon rolled after them, followed by the remaining riders. The doors began to close again.

The convoy came to a halt in the centre of the building. The wagon and its accompanying riders were illuminated by the faint yellow glow of the kerosene lantern. The stables to either side were shrouded in darkness.

At a command from the leader of the party the riders kicked their feet free from the stirrups and prepared to dismount.

Then a harsh voice broke the silence. 'Get down real slow, boys. We've got you covered.'

The members of the Boot Hill Gang looked around them wildly. One of them sent his hand flashing towards his holster.

Half a dozen guns roared in the darkness. The foolish gunman took three or four hits. He toppled off his horse and crashed to the ground, dead as mutton. His horse, frightened by the sound of gunfire, began to rear and plunge wildly.

The man beside him caught a badly aimed shotgun blast full in the face. At that range the shot hadn't even started to spread. Hit by all nine buckshot balls his head flew apart, spraying blood, brains and splinters of bone all over the next man in line.

Half blinded by the flying blood and brains, the gunman dropped his reins and reached towards his pocket for a cloth to wipe away the mess.

It was a fatal mistake. One of George King's men, misinterpreting the gesture as an attept to pull a gun, pumped two .45 slugs into his belly.

The man screamed like a woman as his guts spilled out of his bullet-torn paunch and slithered to the ground. His horse, spooked by the smell of blood and guts, neighed in fright and bucked him out of the saddle. He screamed again as he landed on his face on the rammed earth floor in a tangle of torn intestines.

The four remaining men kept as still as mice. The message was crystal clear.

Make a try for a gun and be shot down like a dog.

The judge stepped from behind an empty stall. His Winchester was tucked casually under his arm. 'Throw down your guns and you won't get hurt!' he said evenly. 'Resist and you'll be shot!'

The members of the Boot Hill Gang exchanged despairing glances, then did as they were told.

When all their weapons had thudded to the floor George King and his men came out of their hiding places. They were grinning all over their faces. For months they had been running scared of the Boot Hill Gang. Now they were starting to fight back!

'Get their guns, Rory,' ordered George. The miner handed his smoking shotgun to his partner, Jacob Ginnel, and came forward holding a burlap sack he had found in an empty stall. He scooped up the discarded rifles and handguns and put them in his sack. Then he stepped back out of the line of fire.

At the judge's command the two surviving riders got down off their horses.

'And you!' he barked, gesturing with his rifle towards the two men seated on the wagon. They hurriedly climbed down to join their collegues. 'We've got a job for you.'

Jolly Jack swaggered forward, grinning all over his face. 'We sure have.' He pointed towards the pile of straw in the corner of the building. 'There's the gold. You came here to take it away. Well, get to it!'

'What if we don't?' one of the gunmen said belligerently. 'Yeah, what if we don't?' one of his companions echoed him defiantly.

'Then we'll shoot you,' George King said coldly. He shrugged his thin shoulders as if he really didn't care either way. 'Why not? You're all gonna die one way or another.'

'Why? We ain't done nothin'.' The teamster was shaking with fear. He could almost feel the rough hemp tickling his neck.

'Don't give me that!' George's voice dripped scorn. 'You stole my gold and killed my men. You'll all hang for that. Tomorrow, if I have my way.'

'Don't we even get a trial?' another gunman protested nervously. He was younger than the others and rather less hard-bitten. 'I didn't kill anyone. I wasn't even in on that raid!'

Jolly Jack laughed unsympathetically. 'But can you prove it, boy?'

The young gunman's face fell. 'I guess not.'

'Then you'll hang with the others!'

Utterly cowed, the four surviving gang members began to load the gold bars into the wagon under the guns of the two miners, Rory and Jacob. The rest of the vigilantes leaned against the timbers of the empty stalls and watched them work. The bars were heavy and the gunmen soon worked up a sweat. But eventually they got the job done.

'Don't forget your friend,' chuckled Jolly Jack as they wiped their streaming brows and stretched their aching backs.

'What friend?' one of them grunted. 'We ain't got no friends here!'

'Oh yes you have.' The store-keeper shone the lantern on Pete's unconscious body lying on a pile of straw in a corner out of the way.

The gunmen's jaws dropped. 'That's Pete! Is he dead?'

Jolly Jack shrugged. 'Who knows! He was alive an hour ago. But alive or dead, get him into the wagon and be quick about it!'

Five minutes later the wagon was again rolling down the street. The two teamsters were on the box. The surviving gunmen sat or lay on the bars of gold in the flatbed.

The two miners, Rory and Jacob, walked behind the wagon keeping their shotguns trained on the gunmen.

The judge, Jack Reeve, George King and two of his men rode beside the wagon on horses captured from the members of the Boot Hill Gang.

They went straight to the livery stable

used by Jolly Jack's stageline, where the gunmen from the Boot Hill Gang sweated to unload the heavy bars of gold from the wagon and reload them into one of Jolly Jack's stagecoaches. Then with one of his trusted shotgun guards on the box beside the driver and four more heavily armed men riding the cushions, the coach set off down the long trail to the county seat.

By now the former members of the Boot Hill Gang were wishing they had never set eyes on the gold. Their backs were breaking and their hands were covered in weeping blisters.

George turned to the judge with a question in his eyes. 'OK. That's the gold taken care of. What do we do with the men?'

'Take them down to the jail, of course,' the judge answered blandly. 'They're Ryker's job now.'

Jolly Jack thought that was very funny. 'Burt Ryker will love that!' he gurgled, slapping his thigh. 'I can hardly wait to see his face.'

'Why's that, Jack?' said George, looking puzzled.

'Oh, come on, George. You know how Ryker hates vigilantes. Leave it to the proper authorities, that's what he says. Meaning him, of course.'

George King nodded. It was true.

'Well, he ain't done much, has he? For all his fine talk. Went out with a posse, caught none of the bad guys and got a few good men killed doing it. We've caught a bunch of 'em and recovered your gold. Makes him look pretty bad, wouldn't you say?'

Put like that, George King had to agree.

By now Pete had recovered his senses. He was untied and helped to his feet.

The judge gestured with his rifle barrel. 'Right, you men. Walk on down to the jail. Any monkey business and you'll get shot.'

The vigilantes and their five prisoners set off down the centre of the street towards the jail. The tired gunmen walked in front, two of them supporting the still-dazed Pete. The judge and his companions walked behind, guns cocked and ready for action. Having caught these men they weren't about to let them go without a fight.

They all knew it might well come to that. Almost anyone in town might be a member of the Boot Hill Gang. And the gang had a reputation for looking after its own.

They didn't expect to get to the jail without being seen. Nor did they. A loafer saw them approaching and dashed into the nearest saloon and gave the alarm. The saloon emptied as the drinkers poured out on to the sidewalk to see the show.

Hearing the noise, men poked their heads out of the next saloon on the strip, and the next and the next. Soon the street was lined with curious and half-drunken men, whooping and calling out damn-fool questions which the judge and his men studiously ignored.

The little band of vigilantes clutched their guns more tightly, their eyes scanning the crowded sidewalks for the first sign of a lifted weapon.

There were a number of Boot Hill Gang members in the crowd of onlookers, but with so many people watching the show rescue was impossible. Anyway, they had no one to tell them what to do. So they scowled at each other and fingered their guns, hoping to God that their unfortunate friends would keep their mouths shut.

Down the street a window on the top floor of the hotel opened without a sound. The occupant of the room rested his rifle on the sill and took careful aim at one of the prisoners. His finger tightened on the trigger.

Crack!

At the sound of the shot the watching men instinctively dived for cover. Out in the centre of the street, the vigilantes had nowhere to hide. They gripped their guns and stared about them wildly.

None of them had been hit. Nor had any of their prisoners.

A rifle slithered down the sloping roof of the hotel and fell into the street.

They all looked up. A man dressed in range clothes was standing at the open window. He was swaying backwards and forwards. Then he folded over the sill and toppled into the street.

The shooting seemed to be over, for the moment. The men on the sidewalk got to their feet. One of them ran over to the body. He struck a match on the seat of his jeans and held it close to the dead man's face. 'It's Johnny Mercer,' he called to his companions in amazement. 'Plugged through the heart.'

There was a murmur of surprise from the watching men. Mercer was known as a sure-thing killer. But who had he been trying to kill? And who had killed *him?*

All eyes turned in the direction from which the shot had come. But there was nothing to be seen except a cloud of powdersmoke hanging in the air by the corner of the Bon Ton saloon. The gunman, whoever he was, had vanished.

The judge smiled to himself. He had wondered where Hunter had got to. Now he knew. The Preacher was still riding shotgun on the little group of vigilantes. It was a comforting feeling.

The door of the sheriff's office burst open and Sheriff Ryker came plunging out, gun in hand. His face showed surprise at the sight of so many men on the sidewalks.

'What's that shooting?' he barked. Then he saw the little group of vigilantes and their prisoners in the centre of the street and instantly lost interest in the shooting. His bushy eyebrows shot up to meet his hatbrim. He glared at the judge.

'Who are these men?' he demanded. 'And why have you got them under the gun?'

Before the judge could reply George King pushed through to the front. 'Members of the Boot Hill Gang,' he crowed. 'You couldn't catch them, but we did! *And* we got my gold back!'

The crowd gasped. The sheriff was rocked back on his heels. 'Whaa . . . ' he stuttered, glaring at the exultant mine-owner.

'That's right,' the judge confirmed. 'We caught them red-handed with the gold. There were eight of them originally. Three tried to fight u . We left their bodies where they fell.

'And where's the gold?'

'On its way to the county seat   le guard.' George King replied smu

'Sheriff, I want you to lock the   nen in jail for the night,' said the judge. 'I'll try them in the morning.'

The crowd cheered loudly. A trial would be something to watch.

Hidden in the crowd, the members of the Boot Hill Gang shifted nervously from foot to foot. Who could tell what these five men might say when they were put on the stand? The thought of a hemp necktie tends to loosen the tongue pretty quickly. Suddenly Texas seemed a mighty attractive place to go on a visit.

Burt Ryker gritted his teeth. The vigilantes had beaten him this time. But the hand was a long way from being played out.

'OK,' he said sullenly. 'Take 'em over to the jail.'

Two men pushed through the crowd. They were carrying the body of the dead rifleman. There was a big splotch of blood on his shirt right over his heart.

Ryker looked at the body in amazement. 'That's Johnny Mercer. How'd he get involved in all this?'

A drunken voice from the crowd called out: 'He tried to bushwhack the judge and his men.'

'But he was plumb out of luck!' another finished cheerfully.

Ryker glared at the judge. 'You shoot him, Judge? Or did one of these *vigilantes* of yours do it?' His voice dripped scorn as he spoke the hated word.

The old man shook his head. 'No. It

wasn't us. We didn't even know he was there. Our guardian angel shot him. And saved our bacon!'

Burt Ryker's mouth twisted as though he'd been sucking on a piece of sour cactus. 'Don't give me that!' he said contemptuously. 'There ain't no damned angels.'

'Don't ferget Angel Horrigan down at Molly's cathouse!' someone yelled from the depths of the crowd. 'She can look after me anytime!'

A roar of laughter went up.

Burt Ryker scowled blackly. This wasn't getting him anywhere. 'Come on then,' he growled unwillingly. 'Bring 'em in to the jailhouse.' He turned to the crowd. 'Go home, you lot! Show's over!'

The five members of the Boot Hill Gang were locked in the cells for the night.

Burt Ryker slumped into his chair and tipped his hat on to the back of his head. He glared at the three townsmen and their gun-toting assistants. 'Think you've done a good job, don't you?'

'Yes. I think so,' said the judge. 'It's a start, anyway.'

'Yeah. The start of real big trouble for Jackpot. You put those gunnies on trial and you'll bring the Boot Hill Gang down on our necks. They've left us alone so far. Maybe they likes to drink and gamble here. Now they'll turn on us.' His mouth twisted cynically. 'Then we'll see whether the good citizens of Jackpot will back you and your damned vigilantes!'

7

At four o'clock the following morning the good people of Jackpot were jerked awake by the sudden roar of gunfire.

They raised their heads from their pillows and listened nervously. From the sound of things a full-scale gunbattle was going on down at the end of the street.

The firing died away. There was a pause, then the listeners heard the sound of five slow, deliberate shots. Shortly after that the clatter of hooves told the townspeople that the gunmen had ridden away and it was safe to go out.

All over town men scrambled into their clothes and leaving their wives and children cowering in their beds, hurried out on to the street.

They realized immediately where the shots had been coming from. The jailhouse door hung open and a thread of powdersmoke was seeping out of the building.

At first no one dared to go into the jail. Then Burt Ryker, burly and unshaven, pushed through the crowd. 'Stand back,' he ordered. 'This is my business!' Drawing and cocking his gun cautiously he stepped inside.

His office was full of thick black smoke, but was otherwise empty.

Ryker strode over to the cells. Last night he had locked the five members of the Boot Hill Gang in there to await trial. He hadn't bothered to lock the front door of the jailhouse when he left the building. He never did.

Maybe he should have done. Someone had entered the building while he was sleeping and shot the five badmen. Their bodies lay tangled on the floor of their cell in a spreading pool of blood.

Then the judge arrived, dressed in a long silk dressing gown. To Ryker's unspoken disgust the new preacher was with him.

'You don't take good care of my prisoners, do you, Ryker!' complained the judge. 'They can't tell us anything now!'

'Then catch some more, seeing as you're so good at it, you and your vigilantes,' sneered Ryker.

He turned his back on the judge and began to usher the crowd out of his office with sweeping gestures of his arms. 'Go home, people. Go home. Show's over!'

His deputy imitated his gestures. 'Sheriff's right!' he drawled. 'Get outa here!'

The crowd slowly drifted away, chattering animatedly amongst themselves.

The Preacher knelt by the bodies. They had been shot to pieces. Then, just to make quite sure that they had been silenced for ever, someone had taken the trouble to put a bullet through each man's head.

The sheriff saw him kneeling by the bodies and assumed that he was praying. 'Yep, there *are* five of 'em,

Preacher,' he said contemptuously. 'Another twenty-five dollars comin' your way.'

He took a cigar from his top pocket and lighted it, then blew a cloud of pungent smoke towards the preacher. 'And *that's* on top of the twenty you'll be gettin' fer the men the judge's vigilantes killed last night. Yer doin' well, ain't yer?'

His eyes narrowed. Come to think of it, over twenty men had died suddenly since the preacher came to Jackpot. Was there a connection?

At first the sheriff had despised the new preacher. He had no time for Bible-bashers. To his mind they were like snake-oil salesmen, all smarmy tongue and greedy hands.

A real man wore a gun and was prepared to defend himself when challenged. Preachers never wore guns. In Ryker's book that made them all cowards.

But since this man Walker came to town the sheriff had been forced to think again. The preacher had stood up to the angry crowd of miners and made them back down, thus preventing a gunfight up at the graveyard. Then he had fought off the six bully-boys who'd invaded his church. He'd had help from Jolly Jack and the judge, but by all accounts he'd played his part like a man.

A light suddenly went on in Ryker's bullet head. A week ago the Boot Hill Gang had got the miners and honest townsmen buffaloed. Now they were fighting back. *Someone* had stirred them up. And who was new in town? The preacher!

The judge touched Hunter's arm. 'Come away, Aaron. There's nothing we can do here.' He nodded to the sheriff. 'See you, Ryker!' then walked away with the black-clad figure of the preacher at his side.

Sheriff Ryker leaned against the doorpost, puffing on his stogie, and watched the two men walk down the street to the judge's house and go inside. His brow was creased in thought. If only he could be sure that the preacher was leading the vigilantes! He'd know what to do then.

The judge and the Preacher went back to sleep. But not for long. At eight o'clock they were having breakfast with Stacy Barton.

The judge wasn't a happy man. He'd hoped the trial would shed some light on the workings of the Boot Hill Gang. He'd planned to offer the five gunmen their lives if they told him who was bossing the gang. But now they were all dead.

'The Boot Hill Gang have beaten us again,' he grumbled.

Hunter's broadcloth-clad shoulders lifted in the faintest of shrugs. 'That's the way it goes,' he said easily. 'We'll get another chance soon. And don't forget, we've hurt them badly. All those men gone and nothing to show for it. George's gold will be halfway to the county seat by now.'

The judge wasn't about to be

placated that easily. 'That's all very well, Hunter. But we still don't know who's bossing that bunch. How are we going to find out, eh?'

His sharp old eyes bored into Hunter's ice-cold grey ones. 'Prisoners, that's what we need. More prisoners. And this time I won't give 'em to Ryker to guard.' His tone made it clear that he blamed Hunter for the men's untimely deaths.

Stacy Barton broke in hastily, 'Don't you think you're being rather unfair, Uncle? Thanks to Mr Hunter here the Boot Hill Gang has already lost its reputation for invincibility. A few more disasters like last night and they'll pack up altogether.'

The judge snorted. 'I'll believe it when I see it. More likely they'll launch a full-scale revenge attack on the town. That's what Ryker thinks, anyway.'

Stacy Barton put up her chin. 'Then give me a gun, Uncle. I can shoot as straight as most men.' Her face clouded over and her voice lost its sparkle as she continued, 'That's what Stephen used to say, anyway.'

Hunter smiled encouragingly at the handsome woman across the table. 'Don't worry, Stacy. I haven't forgotten about your husband. The miners must know something about him. I'll ride into the hills after breakfast and ask them.'

Stacy's face came alive with hope. She put her hand on his sleeve. 'Show them the photograph I gave you. Someone must recognize him! They must. He was here. He wrote and told me so. He'd bought a big mine and it was doing real well!'

Hunter shook his head sadly. 'I asked Mr Sawyer about that, Stacy; even showed him the photo. He didn't recognize your husband.' He paused, then added delicately, 'Maybe he never came here after all.'

'He *was* here,' Stacy insisted mulishly. 'Stephen wouldn't lie to me!'

The glance the judge shot at the Preacher was full of pity and regret.

Unfortunately Stacy saw it. She flushed red, then white. She got to her feet. 'I know you don't believe me, Uncle,' she said between clenched teeth, 'but Stephen is a good man. If he said he he'd bought a claim here, he was telling the truth, and if he's keeping out of sight now it's for a good reason.' She turned to face the Preacher. 'You'll find him, Mr Hunter. I know you will. Then you'll discover that I was right.'

Face set and head held high she swept out of the dining-room.

'Phew!' The judge took out his handkerchief and mopped his brow. 'Women!' he said feelingly. 'Once they've got an idea in their heads it's virtually impossible to get it out again.'

The Preacher got to his feet. 'I know you don't think her husband is any good, Judge,' he said. 'But Stacy loves him, and if a woman like Stacy loves him he can't be *all* bad, can he?'

'Humph!' snorted the judge. 'Call that logic?'

Hunter smiled faintly. 'Of course not. But Stacy won't be happy until she learns the truth. So I'd better go look for him. If he's alive, I'll find him and bring him in. And if he's dead, I'll bring her his body.'

The judge stroked his white beard thoughtfully. 'Just make sure you get back in one piece, that's all I ask. Without you, resistance to the Boot Hill Gang would collapse overnight. That's your main business hereabouts, Hunter; crushing the Boot Hill Gang. Finding Stephen Barton comes a very poor second!'

'Not to Stacy, it doesn't!' said Hunter ruefully, and left the room.

As Hunter rode up the creek towards the workings he was pleased to see that the miners had taken his advice and posted armed guards on the top of the cliffs. As he rode into sight one of them fired a shot into the air to warn the men working up the valley that someone was coming.

The sound of the shot racketed off

the beetling cliffs. Hunter took off his hat and waved it in the air three times. It was the agreed signal. He hoped the riflemen remembered it too.

No shots came his way, so he replaced his hat on his head and kept on riding.

As he rounded an out-thrust spur of rock and rode into the area where the mines were congregated most thickly he felt a surge of disgust at the ruin which mining had brought to this little valley.

Once this must have been a pretty spot, with a sparkling stream flowing through beds of gravel and aspen groves covering the hillsides. Now the trees had all been cut down to build huts and mining equipment.

The stream that ran brawling down the creek was discoloured with mud and crushed minerals. Mine shafts yawned blackly in the hillsides on either side, surrounded by the tumbledown huts of the miners and the strange shapes of the sorting and crushing machinery.

Men worked stripped to the waist, swinging hammers and picks or turning the handles of their homebuilt rock-crushers. Other men wheeled barrowloads of ore out of the dark mineshafts and down to the washing and sorting machinery.

The rumble of iron wheels was loud on the air, but no birds sang. They had all flown away to find unpolluted streams and hillsides where the green grass had not been covered by waste from the mines.

It was a dismal sight.

The trail was rutted and muddy and Hunter's horse had to pick its way slowly and carefully through the mire.

When he arrived in the centre of their encampment a group of miners was waiting. They gathered round him, glad of the excuse to stop work for a minute or two.

'Howdy, Preacher,' one of them said cheerfully. 'What're you doin' here? You ain't plannin' on preachin' to us agin, are yer? It ain't Sunday!'

'You got it wrong, Bill,' another man replied with a grin. 'He wants another scrap with Dutch Bronson.'

'Well, he ain't gettin' one,' growled Bronson. Suddenly his brutal face split in a wry smile. 'No offence, Preacher, but you hit too damned hard.'

Hunter took the photograph of Stephen Barton from his pocket book and held it up. 'I'm looking for this fella,' he said, then leaned down and handed it to the nearest man. 'Take a look and pass it round.'

'What's he done?' someone called from the back of the crowd.

'Vanished!' Hunter replied drily. 'His wife has asked me to help her find him.'

'Maybe *she's* the reason for him vanishin',' a miner sniggered.

'You haven't seen Mrs Barton, or you wouldn't say that,' Hunter answered coldly.

The photograph passed slowly from hand to hand. There was much shaking of heads and muttered denials.

'Surely someone must recognize

him?' said Hunter. He was beginning to lose hope. 'He's supposed to have bought a mine up here. Paid a lot of money for it too.'

'Have you asked Milton Sawyer?' Tin-Cup pushed through the crowd with Gandy Dancer by his side.

'Yes. He said he hadn't seen Barton.'

'Did you believe him?'

'Well . . . ' Hunter shrugged his shoulders. 'I can't say I took to the man. But why should he lie?'

Gandy turned his head aside and spat in the dust. 'I dunno. But I tell you this, Preacher; Sawyer has bought a lot of claims from miners frightened off by the Boot Hill Gang. He don't put up no markers like the Boot Hill Gang do, but a fair few of the empty claims are his now. If we *do* manage to smash the Boot Hill Gang he'll be sitting pretty.'

The photograph of Barton had gone round the group of men without anyone recognizing him. Hunter was about to put it back in his pocket-book when a thought struck him. Maybe one of the wives would recognize it.

Most of the miners' womenfolks lived in town, where they were safe from the Boot Hill Gang, but a few had chosen to stick it out up here with their men.

When he made the suggestion it was greeted with derision by most of the miners. Oddly enough it was Dutch Bronson who shut them up. 'Perhaps *your* women can do nothing but cook and clean,' he growled, 'but mine Bertha is an educated woman. She can read *and* write!' he declared proudly.

He turned and bellowed down the valley. 'Bertha! *Liebchen! Komm hier!*'

A big burly woman came out of Bronson's hut and strode towards them. She was taller than most of the miners and her shoulders were almost as wide as theirs. Two blond pigtails hung down her back.

She pushed through the crowd of grinning men as if they were not there. 'Vot is it, Karl?' she asked.

'The Preacher here is looking for a man,' rumbled Bronson. 'I thought you might have seen him, maybe.'

The woman turned her big blue eyes on Hunter, who touched his hat respectfully.

'You beat my man,' she said flatly.

'So I did,' Hunter replied, meeting her gaze steadily.

'Then you are a man!' She glanced at the other miners contemptuously. 'None of zese poor fish could do it! *Doch!* I could beat them easily mine own self!'

Hunter grinned at her approvingly. She was a fit mate for a man like Bronson. He was willing to bet that the big man didn't have it all his own way at home, either.

'Take a look, Mrs Bronson,' he said, handing her the photograph of Stephen Barton. 'I'd be obliged if you'd show it to the other women too.'

Bertha Bronson tossed her head, setting her long plaits swinging. 'No need,' she said gutturally. 'I know zis man. His name is Clark. Tom Clark. His mine is up zere.'

She waved a flipper-like hand in the direction of the side valley down which Hunter had ridden two nights before. But I have not seen zis man for many weeks. Maybe he is dead.'

At first the miners were unwilling to believe her. 'Tom Clark?' one said scornfully, snatching the photograph from her hand and holding it up for everyone to see. 'That isn't Tom. This fella's a toff! Look at his eyeglass!'

'And Tom had a big, black beard,' another miner declared as if that clinched the matter. 'This man's chin is as smooth as a baby's ass.'

'I guess I knew Tom as well as anyone.' An older man came forward and took the photograph in his work-gnarled hand. He peered at it carefully for a long time. 'Got to make allowance fer this fella not havin' a beard, I guess,' he mumbled to himself.

He handed the photograph back to Hunter, saying thoughtfully, 'Maybe Bertha is right. It *could* be him. But it's plumb hard to tell. This here's a city slicker, right enough. But workin' out here can sure change a man.'

He turned to face the Preacher. 'If it's really Tom you're lookin' for, Preacher, you're wastin' your time. He's dead.' His voice held finality.

'Are you sure?'

'Sure enough. As Bertha just tole yer, Tom's mine was up on Rock Creek. He swore he'd found paydirt and was a-goin' to be rich.'

He shrugged. 'But we all say that, don't we, boys!'

There was a chorus of rueful agreement from the other men. The belief that they would strike it rich any day now was the only thing that kept them going.

'Unlike us fellers, Tom weren't short of a dollar. He bought machinery in town and had it shipped up there, though I never saw any gold goin' the other way. Had three men workin' for him at one time. Hell, I even worked for him myself when times got hard round here, and he paid up on the dot like a Christian.'

'So what happened to him?'

'What the hell d'you think? The Boot Hill Gang, of course!' Gandy Dancer broke in angrily.

The old miner scowled at Gandy. 'You tellin' this, or me?' He spoke directly to Hunter. 'Tom was one of the first to find the devil's cross on his claim. That's the gang's way of givin' yer notice to quit.'

Hunter nodded. 'I know. Go on.'

The old man shrugged. 'Tom wasn't the man to quit a payin' claim just like that. He swore to stay put and his men all said the same. Three nights later the gang attacked 'em.'

'And they were all killed?'

The miner nodded grimly. 'We buried Tom's three men where they fell. There weren't no sign of Tom's body, but the bunkhouse was a burnt-out ruin so we guessed he must have been burned to death inside. None of us fancied lookin' too closely.'

'So he could still be alive?'

The man stroked his chin thought-fully. 'He *could* be, I guess. But if he's still alive why ain't he shown hisself.'

A gabble of agreement from the listening miners showed that they thought the old man had made a telling point.

'So who owns his mine now?' asked Hunter.

The man shrugged. 'Who knows? Tom never said anythin' about havin' a family.'

Tin-Cup chuckled sourly. 'Only a fool would go up there now. The Boot Hill Gang have got their marker on every claim in Rock Creek. They'd shoot anyone who tried to work Tom's claim, or any of the others fer that matter.'

Two or three of the men in the crowd had once had claims in Rock Creek. They confirmed that they had been driven off by the Boot Hill Gang.

'Mind you, I wouldn't go back to Rock Creek now, not if I could pick up nuggets the size of my head,' another man said enigmatically.

Hunter raised his eyebrows. 'Oh! Why's that?'

'The place is haunted!'

'So it is!' a grizzled miner agreed, and he was supported by all the men who had once had claims in Rock Creek.

'Haunted? How?'

'Every now and again one of us rides up on to the caprock and looks down into Rock Creek, makin' sure they ain't workin' our old mines. Mostly we does it of a night-time. Daytime we's workin' our new claims down here in the valley. Waal, Preacher, now and agin we've seen a light moving about way up the creek. Heard strange noises too.'

'Bert's son Brian went up there one day to have a look round, cautious like. He saw nothin'. But he said he felt eyes on his back all the time he was there.'

'Maybe you're right,' Hunter said thoughtfully, tucking the photograph back in his pocket-book. 'But I prefer a simpler explanation.'

He did not elaborate on this statement, but turned and smiled at Mrs Bronson. 'Thank you for your help, madam.'

The big German woman bobbed her head in acknowledgement of the courtesy. By her side, Dutch Bronson looked proud and pleased.

Hunter addressed the other miners. 'And thank you too, gentlemen. Now I mustn't keep you from your work any longer, must I?'

Taking the hint, the miners drifted away.

8

The Preacher went with Gandy and Tin-Cup to their shanty.

'So Tom Clark is really the missing Stephen Barton, Preacher?' the whiskery old miner said knowingly.

'I think so.'

'And he's the ghost?'

'Yes.'

'But why?'

'I don't know. But I do know he's dangerous. I was up there a day or two ago, poking around the abandoned mines. While I was there he did his best to kill me.'

Tin-Cup chuckled richly. 'That ain't so easy, is it, Preacher!'

'Not while the Lord protects me, no,' said the Preacher calmly.

The two miners were not religious men. Hunter's calm assurance of God's favour made them slightly uneasy.

Gandy hurried to change the subject. 'So are you goin' to tell this woman her husband's hidin' in the hills like a crazy man?'

'Not yet, Gandy. He'll keep for a while.'

'What now then?'

Hunter eyed the two men amusedly. 'See what Milton Sawyer has got in his safe.'

Gandy Dancer's pale-blue eyes twinkled with humour. 'Oh yeah! And how you goin' to do that? As if I couldn't guess.'

Tin-Cup rubbed his hands together in glee. 'Wants us to blow it for him, doesn't he!'

The grizzled old miner got to his feet and began filling a sack with tools. A ten-pound maul, three different sizes of cold chisel, a small crowbar, a selection of files. 'Get the bang-sticks, Gandy.'

His partner opened a wooden box on a shelf and took out three sticks of dynamite. 'That ought to be enough,' he cackled.

It was well after dark when the three

men rode into town. They avoided the main street with its busy saloons and honky-tonks. The back streets were dark, which suited them fine.

They dismounted round the back of Sawyer's office. It was locked and dark. Sawyer had a fine house at the other side of town and only used his office during the day.

Gandy Dancer took a small crowbar from the sack of tools and inserted it into the crack between the back door of the building and its frame. Tin-Cup pressed a bundle of cloth over the spot to muffle the sound of splintering wood. Hunter drew his gun and stood on guard.

Gandy leaned his weight on the end of the forged iron bar. For a moment or two he strained against the resistance of the wood, then the doorframe gave way with a muffled crack. The door swung open.

'There you are, Preacher,' snickered Gandy. 'Easy as takin' candy from a baby.'

Hunter led the way inside the building. The moon was up and enough light streamed in through the window for them to be able to see what they were doing.

The safe stood in a corner of the land agent's office. It was a big old thing, almost as high as a man. God knows what it had cost to haul it over the hills from Denver.

'Can you open it?'

The Preacher saw the flash of white teeth as the two miners grinned in the darkness.

'Just watch us!' chuckled Tin-Cup, fumbling in the sack for the ten-pound maul. Then he handed a cold chisel to his partner.

'I allus gets to hold the chisel,' his partner grumbled softly, placing the point of the tool against the top of the combination dial. 'Next time I wants to swing the hammer!'

'Not a chance!' whispered Tin-Cup. 'I need all the fingers I got!'

'Get on with it,' breathed Hunter,

holding back a laugh. 'Save the funnies for later.'

'OK, boss. Ready, Gandy?'

'Ready as I'll ever be.'

Tin-Cup swung the hammer with all his strength. There was a loud ringing sound and the dial broke off and fell to the floor, exposing the mechanism of the lock.

'So far so good!' Gandy repositioned the chisel. Tin-Cup raised the hammer and struck again.

Gandy yelped and wrung his hand, cursing volubly. Both chisel and lock fell on to the safe with a clatter.

Tin-Cup grasped the handle and twisted it firmly but the safe refused to open.

'You clumsy devil,' complained his partner, blowing on his fingers. 'Buckled the locking bars, ain't yer! Now we gotta do this the hard way.'

The whiskery old miner fumbled in the pocket of his coat and took out a stick of dynamite.

'Not a whole stick, surely?' protested

Hunter. 'I hope that safe's full of papers. I don't want them burnt to ashes, you know.'

'Spoilsport,' grunted Gandy. 'I likes a big bang.' But he took out his knife and cut the dynamite in half. 'Mind you, half a stick mightn't be enough to blow that door open.'

'Then you can try a whole stick next time.'

Gandy put the dynamite into the hole and packed it round with glaziers' putty.

'Better take cover!' he said gleefully. 'Behind Sawyer's desk'd be favourite.'

He struck a match on the seat of his pants and touched it to the fuse. It caught at once. As the fire raced spluttering and sparking down the fuse towards the dynamite the old miner scuttled across the room and joined the others behind the solid wooden desk.

The *boom* of the explosion was deafening. The solid iron box, weighing half a ton at least, leapt into the air and toppled over on to its side. The massive iron door burst open, showering papers all over the floor. Some of them were alight, others were smouldering. The room was full of swirling yellow fumes.

Hunter hurriedly picked himself up and, ears ringing, dashed forward to beat at the flames with his hat. Soon the flames were out.

The three men emptied Sawyer's safe and shovelled all the papers into a sack.

'That's the lot. Now let's get out of here before anyone comes to investigate,' said Hunter.

Drawing his gun and earing back the hammer he opened the door an inch or two and peered out. The street seemed deserted. But he knew that wouldn't last for long.

Hunter threw the door wide and ran outside. He hadn't gone two steps when a gun crashed, a tongue of flame lit up the night, and a bullet drilled a hole in the timber siding not an inch from his head.

Diving to the ground, Hunter sent a

snap shot hurtling towards the shadowy alley mouth from which the bullet had come. A loud yelp of pain was followed by a thud as the hidden gunman's pistol hit the ground and the sound of running feet as he made a swift getaway.

'That's torn it!' Hunter cursed softly to himself, as he got to his feet again. The gunman must have seen his face. He would tell Sawyer who had robbed his safe. It was a fair bet that Sawyer would make the obvious assumption that the Preacher was also the man behind the vigilantes.

The three men ran to their horses and spurred out of town. After they'd gone half a mile they slowed their horses to a walk. Turning in their saddles they looked back towards Jackpot. People carrying lanterns were moving about on the street.

'That's stirred 'em up,' chuckled Gandy. 'Do you think Ryker'll raise a posse and come after us?'

'I doubt it,' replied Hunter. 'But we'd

better split up. I'll see you men later.'
He put out his hand and shook first
Gandy's work-roughened mitt, then his
partner's. 'And thanks.'

'*De nada*,' replied Tin-Cup laconically.

His partner laughed. 'We was glad to
do it, Preacher. Sawyer is a louse. I
don't mind bettin' he's tied in with the
Boot Hill Gang somehow. Maybe
there'll be enough in them papers to
nail him.'

'I hope so,' Hunter replied. He
wheeled his horse and trotted back
towards the town.

Hunter slipped back into the
judge's house without being seen by
anyone. Entering the dining-room he
lit the lamp and then emptied his
sack of papers on to the big
mahogany table.

The documents referred to Sawyer's
dealings in land on either side of
Jackpot Gulch and Rock Creek. Most
of them were dated a year or more ago
and were copies of the original bills of
sale.

Turning them over, Hunter discovered that many of these deeds had writing on the back, reassigning them to Milton Sawyer. Others had been declared void, and then re-registered in the name of Jacob Elkington.

Sawyer had admitted buying mines from men who had been frightened off by the Boot Hill Gang. But he'd implied that he'd only bought a few of them.

Plotting Sawyer's and Elkington's holdings on a map of the district, Hunter discovered that between them they now owned most of the mines in Rock Creek. A surprising number of those in Jackpot Gulch were his too.

Hunter took a paper out of his pocket. Compiled by Gandy and Tin-Cup with help from Bronson and the other miners in Jackpot Gulch, it listed all the claims that the Boot Hill Gang had posted after driving their original owners away.

He compared it with the list of Sawyer's and Elkington's purchases. It was a perfect match.

That settled it. Sawyer *alias* Elkington was tied in with the Boot Hill Gang for sure. But was he the boss? And if not, who was? Sheriff Ryker?

The door opened and Judge Chaffee came into the room. His eyes widened when he saw the papers littering his dining-room table.

'What *have* you got there, Aaron?'

The preacher grinned. 'The contents of Milton Sawyer's safe!'

'So it was you blew it open, was it?' The judge shook his head in mock reproof 'Fine behaviour for a man of God, I must say!'

'As you know, I'm no Jesuit,' said Hunter blandly, 'but I'll go along with them this far: sometimes the ends *do* justify the means.'

'What have you found out?'

'In the last couple of months the Boot Hill Gang has killed ten miners and driven another sixteen men off their claims. These papers show that Sawyer now owns every one of those mines. There's got to be a connection between those two facts.'

'I'd say so,' the judge said grimly. 'Now we'd better see if a jury thinks so too!'

'Here's something else I found.' The Preacher flipped a folded document across the table. 'Look at that, Judge!'

The judge unfolded the document. It was a bill of sale on a mine in Rock Creek. The mine had cost $15,000. The deed was made out to a Tom Clark. He turned it over, and saw that the back was blank. The mine had never been resold.

'So?'

'Tom Clark is Stephen Barton. I took his photograph up to Jackpot Gulch earlier today and got a positive identification.'

The judge gaped at him. 'But Sawyer denied ever having seen Stephen.'

'Then he lied, didn't he?'

'Is Stephen still alive?'

'Yes he is. I've seen him.'

'Then why hasn't he come into town?

Doesn't he know Stacy is here, looking for him?'

'He doesn't even know what day it is!'

The judge looked shocked. 'What the hell does that mean?'

'What it sounds like. His mine was raided by the Boot Hill Gang. They killed his men. They thought they'd killed him too. But he got away. I guess he was hit on the head during the fight. Now he's like a crazy man. When I went up there the other day he attacked me and tried to kill me.'

The judge's jaw dropped. 'Not only mad, but dangerous too? Then we'd better not tell Stacy he's still alive. She'd only want you to bring him here so she can look after him properly. She's much better off believing he's dead.'

The Preacher shook his head reprovingly. 'You can't expect me to go along with *that*, Judge. Stephen Barton needs proper care. And Stacy is the right person to give it to him. With God's help she may even be able to nurse him back to sanity.'

'There's always a chance, I guess,' said the judge doubtfully. 'All right, I'll play along. So where is he living now?'

'In the mine. The other miners think it's haunted.' The Preacher grinned unexpectedly. 'Oh, and there's one more thing: God has smiled upon him in his time of trouble. His mine is brim-full of high-grade ore. It's the richest strike I've ever seen.'

At that moment the door opened and Stacy Barton entered the room. 'Good evening, Uncle, Mr Hunter,' she said in her soft and musical voice. 'Have you got any news for me about Stephen?'

The judge sprang to his feet with an alacrity that belied his years and put an arm round her shoulders. 'Indeed he has,' he said gruffly. 'Stephen is alive and . . .' He broke off in some confusion.

Stacy Barton gave a little shriek of joy. '*Alive!*' Then she realized that something was wrong. Her face fell and she put out a trembling hand towards the Preacher. 'What does Uncle mean, Mr Hunter? Is Stephen ill or something?'

'Please sit down, Mrs Barton,' said Hunter evenly.

Dazed, she did as she was told. The Preacher told her everything he knew and most of what he guessed.

When he'd finished Stacy Barton reached out and grasped the Preacher's hands and pressed them fervently. 'Oh! Thank you, Mr Hunter! Thank you! Thank you! I knew you'd find him.'

She sprang to her feet. 'Rock Creek, you said? I must go there right away. Will you have a buckboard harnessed for me, Uncle?'

Without giving the judge a chance to reply she turned back to Hunter and said excitedly, 'You'll come with me, won't you, Mr Hunter?'

The Preacher hated to damp down so much enthusiasm, but it had to be done. 'No one is going out there at this time of night, Mrs Barton, least of all you,' he said firmly. 'It'd be much too risky. Anyone riding up there tonight is liable to get shot, either by the Boot Hill Gang or by the miners themselves.'

'I'll risk it!' insisted Stacy. 'Stephen might get killed before I have a chance to find him!'

Hunter remembered the fight in the pitch-black mineshaft. 'He'll be safe enough, Mrs Barton. He's living in a mine, remember. *His* mine. No one with any sense is going to follow him down there.' He chuckled mirthlessly. 'But if they do, they surely won't come out again.'

Stacy found his tone reassuring, even if his words were grim. 'All right, I'll do as you say,' she replied reluctantly. 'But you promise to take me up there as soon as the fight's over?'

'I do,' Hunter said flatly.

'Then I'll go to bed.'

She said goodnight to the judge. Then to Hunter's surprise and embarrassment she leaned over and gave him a quick kiss on the cheek. 'Goodnight, Mr Hunter. And thank you!' With a swirl of her skirts she was gone.

9

Next morning, after breakfast, Judge Chaffee made out a warrant for Sawyer's arrest. He also drew up a number of 'John Doe' warrants for the other members of the Boot Hill Gang. Their names would be filled in later.

The Preacher strapped on his gun and pinned his deputy US marshal's badge on to his coat. As marshal he had the authority to arrest wrongdoers wherever he found them. If Sheriff Ryker tried to interfere, the badge might make him think twice.

There had been nothing in Sawyer's safe to tie the sheriff in with the Boot Hill Gang, but neither the judge nor Hunter trusted him an inch.

By ten o'clock the vigilantes had assembled in the judge's house.

Jolly Jack Reeve was there, cracking jokes as he passed out 10-cent cigars to friends and strangers alike. A gunbelt circled his expansive waist and he had tucked a shiny new rifle under his arm. He had brought three of his stagecoach guards with him. They carried Greener shotguns in addition to their belt-guns.

George King had brought the five men who had proved so handy last time they'd met up with the Boot Hill gang.

Gandy and Tin-Cup led a group of miners, all armed to the teeth and eager to avenge themselves on the men who had killed some of their friends and driven others from their claims. A couple of townsmen, friends of the judge, had also been invited to join the vigilantes.

The judge's servant had been watching Sawyer's house since before sun-up. Now he came running back to the house.

'Sawyer ain't gonna wait for you to come and get him, Judge,' he gasped. 'He's coming to get you instead. And it looks like he's got the whole damn Boot Hill Gang with him!'

The vigilantes rushed to the windows and peered out. Sure enough, a bunch of gunmen were swaggering down the street from the direction of Sawyer's house. There were more than twenty of them already, and every saloon they passed contributed a few more.

The land agent was leading them. By gathering all the gang together in broad daylight he aimed to overawe the town and squash any thoughts the citizens might have of avenging the judge's and the Preacher's deaths. Then, with the townsfolk buffaloed and the vigilantes leaderless, he would be able to make himself king of Jackpot.

As the bunch of desperadoes strutted down the street the sidewalks cleared like magic. Idlers found business elsewhere. Gossiping women grabbed their children and hurried them inside their houses. Shopkeepers pulled down their shutters and prepared for the worst.

The band of gunmen halted just out of pistol range and went into a huddle round Sawyer. The portly land agent waved his arms expressively as he gave them their orders.

Inside the judge's house, the vigilantes exchanged nervous glances. What had they got themselves into? There was a small army of badmen out there. They were outnumbered and outgunned. All their eyes turned towards the preacher.

'Well, gentlemen!' he said grimly. 'You can see what we're up against. More than likely some of us are going to die before this is all over.'

A shiver ran through the group of men.

'Some of you have got wives and children. You may feel your first duty is to them. Well, I can understand that. So if anyone wants to leave they may do so now.'

In the silence that followed Hunter eyed his little band of supporters speculatively. Who would stick? The judge, of course. Jolly Jack Reeve. George King and his men. Gandy and

Tin-Cup. But who else?

He had another problem too. Stacy Barton! The judge's house was no place for a woman. Not with a fight to the death about to start.

The judge had been thinking along the same lines. 'You'd better get out of here, Stacy. Robins will take you out the back way. Mrs Klesmer will look after you. Stay at her place until this is all over.'

His niece put up her chin. 'And what if Sawyer's men found me there? He'd use me against you, you know he would. I'm better off here.'

The judge looked nonplussed. Hunter hid a smile. This was one feisty woman.

Dutch Bronson cleared his throat noisily. 'So you will be staying with us, Mrs Barton?' he rumbled.

Stacy smiled wryly. 'Where else could I go?'

'Then we will stay also.'

The other vigilantes were in full agreement with the big miner. They grasped their guns more firmly, resolved to protect the beautiful young woman from the gunmen of the Boot Hill Gang even if it cost them their lives.

Stacy turned her sparkling blue eyes on Dutch Bronson. 'Thank you, Mr Bronson,' she said softly. 'That was very gallant of you.'

The giant miner flushed brick-red under his tan and looked down at his feet.

The judge's house was two storeys high and occupied a corner plot. Its front windows commanded the street. There was a good field of fire at the back too.

Hunter sent his men to their positions, telling them to keep out of sight until the badmen outside the house decided to open the ball.

Sawyer's first move was to send a dozen men round to the back of the house. They kicked open the doors of a couple of abandoned shanties and went inside. They rested their rifle barrels on the rotting windowsills and pointed them towards the house.

At a word from Sawyer his remaining men spread out to cover the front and side of the house. The watching Hunter counted more than twenty of them.

Backed by four of his handiest men, Sawyer strolled across the street and knocked at the judge's door. He had no idea that the judge's house was packed with vigilantes. He thought the house was empty but for the judge, his servant, Stacy Barton and the Preacher. He was in for a big surprise.

'Will you answer the door?' Hunter drawled, drawing and cocking his Colt .44.

'Be rude not to,' the judge replied with a grin, earing back the hammers of his expensive Eastern-made shotgun. He nodded to show that he was ready. Hunter turned the knob and threw the door wide open.

Sawyer and his four men were standing on the step with their guns drawn. They had hoped to catch whoever came to the door by surprise. Instead they were facing a shotgun and a Colt .44. It was a stand off . . . for the moment at least.

Sawyer was undisturbed. 'Howdy, Judge,' he said coolly. 'Been expecting me?'

'After last night you only had two choices,' the judge replied evenly. 'Ride out of here or try and kill me. I knew which one you'd choose.'

'Damn right!' snarled Sawyer. A fleck of spittle appeared at the corner of his mouth. He put out his tongue and licked it away. 'What are two more deaths to me? I'd kill everyone in Jackpot if I had to. The gold in these hills is *mine*!'

For a split second the Preacher could see the Devil looking out of the land agent's eyes. Then Sawyer blinked and the red glare was gone.

The badge on Hunter's coat caught Sawyer's eye. 'So you're a lawman, eh!' he said accusingly. 'Not a preacher after all!'

'You're wrong, Sawyer!' Hunter replied blandly. 'I'm both a lawman *and* a preacher.'

One of Sawyer's sidekicks suddenly pulled at his master's sleeve. 'Then this man's name ain't Walker, boss! It's Hunter!'

'So what?' sneered Sawyer.

The man released his grip on his boss's sleeve and took a step back. His face had gone white. 'You must have heard of the Preacher, boss! He's hell on wheels with a gun!'

'Maybe so.' Milton Sawyer could see no reason to be worried. 'But he's only one man, however good he is, and we've got thirty!'

He gestured expansively towards the gunmen lining the opposite side of the street. They grinned at Hunter and the judge and hefted their weapons.

'I hear you got a woman staying with you, Judge,' Sawyer went on greasily. 'If we have to come in and get you she might get hurt. But if you and this clerical gunfighter of yours agree to give up your guns and come out quietly we'll leave her alone.' He paused expectantly. 'Is it a deal?'

'Hell, no!' said the judge. 'If you want us, you'll have to come in and get us.'

'You're making a big mistake,' grated Sawyer. Behind his back he made a chopping motion with his left hand.

A rifleman positioned on the roof of a building across the street saw the signal, took aim and fired. His bullet smashed into the judge's right shoulder, spinning him round and throwing him against Hunter.

The judge was no lightweight and the Preacher staggered under the impact. This was surely God's hand at work, for if the Preacher hadn't already been moving the rifleman's second bullet would have ploughed right through his heart.

'Get 'em, boys,' yelled Sawyer, stepping back a pace and drawing his gun.

Before his men could obey his command there was a shattering *boom!*

and the front left-hand window of the judge's house blew out in a shower of glass and number 4 shot. Jolly Jack had fired off both barrels of his shotgun with deadly effect.

One of Sawyer's four companions toppled to the ground, spouting blood from a ragged stump where his head had been. The man who had been standing next to him staggered away from the fight, screaming like a pig with its throat cut, quilled like a porcupine with slivers of glass from the broken window.

Enraged by the deaths of their companions the members of the Boot Hill Gang triggered their guns and sent a stream of lead hurtling towards the house.

Sawyer always gave the impression of being a fat man, but much of his bulk was actually solid muscle.

As the shotgun fired, Sawyer stepped neatly behind the man on his left, a small man with striped pants and a fancy vest, and struck his arm a numbing blow with the side of his hand. The gunman screeched and dropped his six-gun.

Sawyer clamped his arm round the man's waist and swung him off his feet, then using the struggling man's body as a shield he scuttled back across the street.

It was a clever move. Two bullets thumped into the hapless gunman's body before they reached the safety of an open doorway, but Sawyer himself was unhurt.

The wounded gunman kicked feebly in Sawyer's grasp. 'Lemme go!' he cried furiously. 'I'm gonna kill you for that!'

'The hell you are!' Chuckling with delight at his own cleverness Sawyer shifted his grip and tossed the helpless man into the street.

As he'd hoped, the vigilantes thought this was the start of another attack and a storm of shot smashed the unfortunate gunman to the ground.

The fourth member of Sawyer's party had met the same fate as his former companions. He was lying on the sidewalk outside the judge's house, leaking blood from a dozen wounds on to the scuffed wooden planks.

The other members of the Boot Hill Gang had hurriedly taken cover wherever they could find it.

Cord Newman and two of his buddies hid behind a wagon that had been standing outside one of the town's general stores a little further down the street. Its driver had run for his life when he heard the first shot.

The burst of gunfire had frightened the horses. They were rearing and plunging between the shafts. Newman drew his Green River knife and slashed at the harness. Half a dozen swipes freed the horses. Eyes rolling in terror they dashed off down the street.

The three men's bodies were safe behind the wagon, but their legs were not. A storm of bullets from the house kicked up sand around the gunmen's boots and plucked at their trouser-legs.

Newman put his shoulder to the

nearest wheel. 'Come on! Let's tip it over,' he yelled to his companions.

The three men clutched at the weatherbeaten woodwork and heaved with all their strength. The wagon rocked, tilted, then crashed back on to the sand.

Two more gunmen were cowering in a nearby doorway. They had tried and failed to kick the door in. The wagon looked a much better bet. Taking advantage of a lull in the firing they made a dash for it.

Inside the judge's house, George King had been waiting patiently for someone to show himself. Now he snuggled his rifle into his shoulder, drew a bead on one of the running men and gently squeezed the trigger.

Hit in the chest, the man spun round, blood pouring from his open mouth, and fell to the ground.

His companion was luckier, reaching the shelter of the wagon unscathed despite the storm of shot that whistled past his ears.

Exerting all their strength, the four gunmen managed to overturn the wagon. They huddled behind the thick oak timbers, gasping for breath. For the moment at least they were safe.

The rest of the gang found refuge in the houses, kicking open the doors and bursting inside, guns cocked and ready for action.

The townsmen and their families cowered away from the wild-eyed gunmen. But the badmen had no interest in these terrified sheep. They herded the frightened men, women and children into their back yards and told them to vamoose. Then they smashed the windows facing on to the street with their gunbarrels and made themselves comfortable with chairs and cushions. From the look of things it was going to be a long siege.

The vigilantes across the street were feeling pleased with the way things had gone. They had killed a number of Sawyer's men at no loss to themselves.

The men at the back of the house

were feeling left out of all the action. 'It's not fair!' called Jolly Jack Reeve. 'You boys are having all the fun!'

'I dare say you'll get your chance soon enough,' Hunter replied drily.

He was right. Sawyer had realized he'd have to rethink his tactics. The judge had more men with him than he'd bargained for. He sent new orders to the gunmen at the back of the house.

The man in charge there was a hard-bitten Missourian named Marvin Hackstead. He had ridden with Quantrill in the War Between the States. He had killed men, women and children in the name of the South. Now he was doing it for pay.

Some of his men were veterans of the war. Others were young firebrands seeking to make themselves a reputation. But they all had one thing in common: they killed for a living and were mighty good at it too.

Hackstead sent two of his men running off down the street. A few minutes later they returned, pushing an empty wagon. They lined it up facing the judge's back gate.

Leaving four men behind with rifles to cover them when they made their attack, Hackstead took his five remaining men to join the two others sheltering behind the wagon.

A sudden burst of shooting from the front of the house told Hackstead that Sawyer was making the promised diversion.

'Right, boys! Push!' he commanded. The gunmen put their shoulders to the wheel. The wagon slowly began to move. Accelerating all the time, it rolled into the judge's back yard.

The defenders were caught by surprise. Hastily they swung up their rifles and fired at the men pushing the rapidly accelerating wagon, but the bullets thumped harmlessly into the stout timbers.

The men at the windows of the tumbledown shanties fired back as fast as they could work the levers on their Winchesters. In seconds every pane of glass at the back of the house was in splinters.

The wagon crashed into the judge's back door and smashed it in. Marvin Hackstead leaped through the shattered doorway, guns blazing. His men followed him eagerly. Pretty Stacy Barton was somewhere in the house; each man wanted to be the first to find her.

One of the miners had been standing behind the door when the wagon hit the house and had been knocked flying. Shocked and bleeding, he staggered to his feet and was promptly shot dead by the grinning Hackstead. The other gunmen jumped over his body and plunged into the house.

Throwing open the first door on the left, three of Hackstead's gunmen burst into the kitchen, looking for action.

They sure found it. Jolly Jack Reeve and one of his teamsters had been positioned at the kitchen window. Both men were toting shotguns. Firing from the hip, they let the onrushing gunmen have all four barrels.

The storm of shot from Jolly Jack's weapon tore into the leading gunman and nigh-on cut him in half. The second man was equally unlucky, the double load of heavy lead balls from the teamster's gun smashing into his checked shirt and throwing him to the ground in a spreading pool of blood.

The third man threw himself to the floor as he heard the quadruple *boom!* and the stream of lead passed safely over his head. Rolling on to his back he raised his gun and triggered two .45 bullets at the closer of his two opponents.

Hit in the belly by both of the spinning lumps of lead, the teamster screamed like a woman and slumped to the floor. Mouth twisted in triumph, the gunman put a third bullet into the writhing man's head.

Meanwhile Jolly Jack had been feverishly thumbing shells into his shotgun. Now he snapped the weapon shut and cocked the hammers.

By now the little room was almost

completely full of choking black powdersmoke. Neither man could see the other properly.

Sawyer's man raised himself on his elbows and shot where he thought his one remaining enemy might be.

It was a good guess, for the bullet hit Jolly Jack in the thigh. But it was also a fatal mistake. The tongue of flame from the gunman's pistol showed the stagecoach owner where to fire. Pointing his shotgun into the rolling smoke Jolly Jack let off both barrels at once. At such close range the gunman was shredded by the torrent of shot.

Dropping his shotgun, Jolly Jack staggered over to the window and threw it wide to disperse the billowing smoke. Then he took a handkerchief from his pocket and tied it tightly round his sluggishly bleeding thigh.

The fire from the house died away as the men inside turned away from the windows to meet the threat from Hackstead and his men.

The four gunmen Hackstead had left

behind in the shanties lowered their weapons. The battle was almost over, or so it seemed. If so, why shouldn't they go across and join in the looting? Maybe they'd even get a turn with pretty Stacy Barton.

Leaving the shelter of the shanties they ran across the open yard towards the house.

It was a mistake they would never have a chance to regret. Mush Morton, the saddler, was one of Judge Chaffee's closest friends. He had been a sharp-shooter in the war. Hunter had positioned him at one of the upstairs windows overlooking the yard. With his first two shots he killed two gunmen. His third shot wounded another man in the shoulder.

The only one of the four gunmen to make it into the house ran down the central corridor and burst into the judge's front room, gun in hand.

The room was full of vigilantes. They were busily firing at the men across the street and didn't notice at first that an enemy had come to join them. The gunny had time to shoot two men in the back before falling victim to Dutch Bronson's old but still serviceable Colt Dragoon pistol.

Hackstead had four men left. Plunging into the room on the right of the passage they shot and killed three miners at the cost of a couple of fleshwounds apiece.

Then they went looking for more enemies to kill. Running along the corridor with his men close behind him Hackstead threw open a door on his left and burst inside, his gun raised and ready to fire. But the room was empty.

In the room on the opposite side of the passage Hunter and Stacy were busy bandaging the judge's wounded shoulder. A bowl of reddish water, some bloody cloths and Hunter's razor-sharp Bowie knife, its blade scarlet, rested on the fine mahogany table. Hunter had just finished digging the bullet from the ragged wound. Halfway through this rough surgery the judge had fainted.

The Preacher and his beautiful companion heard the sudden burst of firing at the back of the house, then the rush of feet in the corridor and the crash as the door of the room across the way was thrown open.

'We'll be next,' whispered the Preacher. 'You'd better get under the table!'

'Not on your life!' Stacy Barton replied fiercely. 'Give me a gun, Mr Hunter. At this range I can shoot as well as any man!'

Hunter shrugged. He couldn't force her to take cover, could he? And he admired her spirit. Stephen Barton was a lucky man. Stacy Barton was a real frontier wife.

'Here you are,' he said wryly, handing her his Winchester repeater. 'And may God defend you!'

Stacy Barton took the weapon and worked the lever expertly, jacking a shell into the breech. Raising the rifle to her shoulder she pointed it towards the door.

Hunter drew his Colt .44. If they wanted to get to Stacy they would have to go through him.

There was a crash and the door burst open. Hackstead and his men rushed in.

He saw Hunter and swivelled to face him, but before he could pull the trigger Hunter shot him right between the eyes. The back of Hackstead's head blew off in a shower of blood and brains that painted the opposite wall with red slime.

Hunter's second shot got the next man in the chest. The gunman slumped to the ground, blowing bloody froth from a punctured lung.

The remaining three men scrambled past the falling bodies of their friends and dove left and right.

Hunter turned on his heel and threw down on a young, hard-faced gunny who was attempting to draw a bead on him. The man screamed as two .44 slugs opened his belly.

Behind him Hunter could hear

Stacy's Winchester spitting out bullet after bullet. He could only hope that they weren't heading in his direction. But at least it proved that she was still alive.

A thin, wiry gunman in a fancy vest swung his gun into line and squeezed the trigger once, twice, as he ducked for cover behind one of the judge's overstuffed chairs. The first shot screamed past Hunter's head. The second burned his ribs.

The Preacher fanned his gun and emptied it into the back of the chair. The horsehair stuffing hardly slowed the bullets at all. Hit by two of the spinning lumps of lead the gunman reared up and fell on to his side, stone dead.

That left one man unaccounted for. But the Preacher's gun was empty. Dropping the useless weapon he dived to the floor and scooped up the dead man's pistol.

But he didn't need it after all. The firing had stopped.

Looking up, he saw Stacy Barton staring blankly across the table. His Winchester drooped from her pretty white hands, a wisp of smoke curling from its muzzle. The fifth gunman was slumped against the wall, stone dead. Stacy had put five or six bullets through his body.

Hunter walked over to her and gently took the Winchester from her hands. 'It's all right, Stacy,' he said softly. 'It's all over.'

Without saying a word Stacy lowered her head until it rested on the Preacher's broad chest. Tears spilled slowly from her eyes and ran down her cheeks.

A groan from the other end of the room informed them that the judge had returned to consciousness at last.

Stacy hurriedly stepped away from Hunter. She fished in her pocket and took out a dainty lace handkerchief and dabbed at her eyes.

'You *have* been having yourselves a time!' croaked the judge, staring at the bodies of the five dead gunmen that lay sprawled in death on his expensive Turkey carpet.

'It did get a bit hectic for a moment there,' agreed Hunter. 'But with God's help we both came through unscathed.'

10

A rattle of shots from the front of the house reminded the Preacher that the battle was far from over. 'I must go.'

'So you must.' The judge hefted his shotgun in his left hand. 'We'll be OK, won't we Stacy?'

The young woman picked up another discarded pistol. 'Don't worry, Mr Hunter,' she said with the ghost of a chuckle. 'I'll look after Uncle.'

'I'm sure you will.'

Hunter recovered his own pistol and reloaded it with shells from his gunbelt; then, thumbing shells into his Winchester as he went, left the room, shutting the door behind him.

He visited each of the remaining rooms in turn. Only four of the vigilantes had been killed so far. Half a dozen of the others had suffered minor wounds.

The Boot Hill Gang had been much less fortunate. Hunter estimated that they had lost almost half their strength already.

It was time to go on the attack.

Posting a couple of men at the back of the house to replace the ones that Hackstead and his men had killed, the Preacher ran across the yard and vanished out of the gate.

Crash!

Cord Newman and his three buddies dived to the ground as a heavy bullet burst through the thick oak timbers of the upturned wagon they were sheltering behind. Fifteen seconds later it happened again, spraying them with sharp splinters.

Newman gave vent to a string of heartfelt curses. One of the men in the house had got a Sharps Buffalo gun or something similar. At this range those thumb-sized bullets would go through the timbers of the wagon like a dose of salts. Sooner or later either he or one of his men would be hit.

'We better make a run fer it, boys,' he grunted, and the others agreed that it would be madness to stay where they were.

The four gunmen waited for the next lull in the firing and then ran for the shelter of the nearest house with bullets kicking up sand all round their flying feet.

But when they got there the door refused to open. The householder had locked and barred it before escaping through the back with his family.

The panic-stricken gunmen pumped shot after shot into the wood around the keyhole in an attempt to break the lock, but without success. And all the time the vigilantes were directing a torrent of shot at them.

First one man slumped to the ground, leaking blood, then a second. Desperate now, Cord Newman dived head-first through a nearby window. The glass cut his face to ribbons but at least he was safe from the vigilantes' bullets. The fourth man tried to follow his lead, but as he ran towards the window a bullet from George King's rifle hit him between the shoulder-blades. Badly wounded, but still alive and fully conscious, the gunman folded forward over the windowsill and screamed as the jagged tongues of glass pierced his belly and thighs.

The Preacher crept up to the back of one of the houses a little further down the street and flattened himself against the rough wooden planks. From the sounds of gunfire and the rumble of coarse voices he could tell that there were at least three men inside the house.

He quietly opened the door and slipped inside. The kitchen was on his left. It was empty. So were the two small rooms facing the yard. He tiptoed down the passage. The door through into the front room was open wide. Through it he could see two gunmen. They were holding rifles and looking out of the windows with their backs to him. The third gunman was standing at a table over to his left. He had a cup of coffee in his hand.

Hunter stepped into the room. 'Drop the guns!' he barked.

The two men by the windows let their rifles fall to the floor. They knew Hunter had the drop on them. The third man was young and foolish. He thought he could beat a drawn and levelled gun. He dropped his coffee cup and reached for his pistol.

He never made it. Hunter swung his Winchester round and shot him through the heart. The other two men seized the opportunity to go for their beltguns. A moment later the little room echoed to the roaring of guns.

When the smoke cleared, both men were down and dead. Hunter had taken a bullet through the left thigh. The wound bled like a pig, but wasn't too serious. Unfastening his black string tie he used it as a tourniquet.

Taking off his hat he placed it on his rifle barrel and held it up at the window. It was the agreed signal. A storm of cheering from the judge's house across the street told him that it had been seen and understood.

In the next house but one, Sawyer heard the cheering and guessed what it meant. Step by step the vigilantes were winning their battle. Soon the towns-people would rediscover their courage and join in. Then he would be finished.

The land agent decided to get out right away, without telling any of his men that he was going. He had a sack of money up at his house that was more than enough to set him up in style anywhere in the West.

The vigilantes fired again, a rolling thunder of sound, and bullets lashed the houses where their enemies were sheltering. The men of the Boot Hill Gang fired back furiously.

Sawyer tiptoed out of the room. The four gunmen sharing it with him hardly noticed he'd gone. Passing silently through the remainder of the house the land agent reached the back door and pushed it open a crack.

Peering out, Sawyer could hardly believe his eyes. His enemy's black-clad figure was less than ten yards away. The Preacher had his ear pressed to the door of the next house along the street. His Winchester leaned against the clapboard wall beside him. His back was towards Sawyer.

The land agent was no gunfighter. He paid other men to die for him. But this chance was too good to miss.

He drew his gun, cocked it quietly and levelled it at the Preacher's unsuspecting back. His finger tightened on the trigger . . .

Crack!

Instinctively the Preacher leapt away from the door and threw himself to the ground, hastily drawing his gun. Then he realized that the shot hadn't been aimed at him. He looked up, feeling foolish.

Ten yards away the tubby figure of Milton Sawyer lay bleeding its lifeblood into the sand. A silver-mounted Merwin and Hulbert pistol lay on the ground by his outstretched hand.

Fifty yards off, Sheriff Ryker was blowing into the muzzle of his smoking Winchester 'Yellow Boy' carbine with the air of a man who has done a good job and knows it. A gang of townsmen stood behind him. They were all carrying guns of one sort or another.

Hunter slowly got to his feet, holstered his pistol, brushed himself down, recovered his hat and clapped it on his head, then picked up his rifle and limped towards Ryker and the group of townsmen.

The sheriff showed his teeth in a grin that was like a juicy slice of water-melon. 'I just remembered where I seen you before, mister,' he said smugly. 'Your name's not Walker, it's Hunter!'

'That's right.'

'Deputy US Marshal!'

'That too.'

'Then why didn't you tell me you was operatin' in my territory?'

Hunter smiled cynically. 'Come on, Ryker. You know the answer to that!'

'I guess I do!' said Ryker flushing an unlovely red. 'But I did what I could, Marshal. Honest!' He shrugged his burly shoulders. 'All right, it seems you done better. But you had to set up a gang of vigilantes ter help you. I wouldn't do that. Vigilantes work outside the law. When you got vigilantes, next thing you know you got lynchings.'

Hunter nodded. The man had a point. The vigilantes had saved Jackpot. In other towns the cure had been worse than the disease.

Ryker had managed to keep the town reasonably quiet, despite the efforts of Sawyer's gunmen to turn it into a hell on earth. He deserved credit for that.

He deserved credit for something else, too. Hunter put out his hand. 'You saved my life,' he said gravely, 'and I thank you.'

Sheriff Ryker gave an elaborate shrug. 'T'weren't nothing,' he mumbled.

'It is to me,' replied Hunter. 'Now,

let's get on with the job of clearing out the remaining members of the Boot Hill Gang.'

The townsmen waved their guns and gave a cheer. Hearing the shooting and realizing that this was their chance to strike back against the Boot Hill Gang they had come to Ryker and demanded that he lead them into action. After all, they said, he *was* Sheriff of Jackpot.

Ryker had been hoping for a chance like this. He had deputized all the able-bodied men in town and led them up the street to rescue the judge and his allies from Sawyer and his gunmen.

Under Ryker's leadership the townsmen cleared the town of gunmen house by house. Fighting continued for a while, but with Sawyer dead the Boot Hill Gang was leaderless, and by midday the remaining gunmen were either dead or had surrendered.

Armed townsmen joined the triumphant vigilantes in escorting the surviving gunmen down the street to the jail and locking them in. By the time they'd done the little jail was bursting at the seams.

The mortician and his assistant had worn themselves out collecting bodies and taking them down to the funeral parlour and they still had a long way to go. There were dead men in the houses, dead men on the street and dead men littering the judge's fine mansion.

Ryker and the Preacher walked down the street together. 'Come and look at this,' said Hunter, leading the sheriff into one of the houses.

Three bodies lay on the floor. Hunter turned one of them over with his boot. It was Deputy Zack Burns.

'Hell!' gasped Ryker. 'So *that's* why the Boot Hill Gang always knew what we was doin'.'

'And why they were able to kill our prisoners in your jail so easily.'

Next day after breakfast Hunter borrowed the judge's buckboard and took Stacy Barton out to the Rock Creek mine. Stacy raised her eyebrows when he saw him tie his own horse on behind, but said nothing.

Hunter did not bother to explain. Before breakfast he had spent some time on his knees. If God answered his prayers he would be needing his horse later on.

When they reached the mine he helped Stacy to dismount and led her across the uneven ground to the mouth of the shaft.

'Call your husband,' he urged her. 'Call him now. If he's in there he'll hear you.'

Stacy plucked up her courage. 'Stephen,' she cried. 'It's me, Stacy! You don't need to hide in there any more. The Boot Hill Gang has been broken.'

There was no reply, but stones rattled inside the mine as if someone had shifted his feet uncertainly.

'Stephen? Stephen, I love you. Come to me. Come to me.'

Stones rattled again, and then a dark figure appeared at the mouth of the mine. He stared at the beautiful young woman in silence for what seemed like an age. Then he dropped the knife he had been holding in his hand. Giving a great cry of wonder and joy, he rushed forward and clasped his wife in his arms.

Stephen Barton was hairy and filthy and stank like a polecat, but Stacy didn't mind a bit. She had her husband back at last.

Hunter's hand hovered over his gunbutt as he watched the two of them embrace. Stephen Barton had been both mad and very dangerous. Maybe he still was.

Stephen Barton eventually opened his arms and released his wife from his embrace. Still holding her hand, he turned to face the black-clad preacher. His eyes were sparkling with intelligence. There was no sign of the homicidal maniac who had attacked Hunter only a few days before. Seeing his wife had obviously restored him to sanity.

'Thank you for bringing Stacy up here, Mr . . . '

'Hunter,' replied the Preacher. 'It was my pleasure.' He gestured towards the buckboard. 'Do you feel up to driving back to town, Mr Barton?'

Stephen Barton's ragged beard opened in a broad smile. 'I sure do,' he said, putting his arm round his wife's waist and giving her a squeeze. She smiled back at him fondly. She seemed to have forgotten that Hunter even existed. Her eyes were only for her husband.

'Then I'll leave you to it.'

Hunter unhitched his horse, swung into the saddle and with a wave of the hand, rode off down the track.

The buckboard reached town more than an hour after him.

The Preacher remained in Jackpot for another week. He had a deal of funerals to conduct. Four of the vigilantes had died in the gunbattle. So had two of the townspeople. There were also twenty-four dead gunmen to bury.

★　★　★

At last it was all over.

Hunter made his farewells and rode out of town, setting his horse at the long slope that led up through the wooded hills towards the snow-capped mountains. He had had more than enough of the reek of gunsmoke and the smell of freshly spilled blood. He was aiming to spend a few weeks in the peace and quiet of the high country, living off the land and communing with his God.

THE END

MIDNIGHT LYNCHING

Terry Murphy

When Ruby Malone's husband is lynched by a sheriff's posse, Wells Fargo investigator Asa Harker goes after the beautiful widow expecting her to lead him to the vast sum of money stolen from his company. But Ruby has gone on the outlaw trail with the handsome, young Ben Whitman. Worse still, Harker finds he must deal with a crooked sheriff. Without help, it looks as if he will not only fail to recover the stolen money but also lose his life into the bargain.